THE R[...]

Local Geologist R[...]

Nevada's Black Rock Desert has always been both a fascinating and forbidding place, drawing some to its stark beauty, others to its solitude. Native Americans have long withdrawn here on spiritual quests, but the desert has never been considered a great vacation destination. Still, the sheriff's office at Gerlach has reported a surprising increase in trekkers registering with them before venturing into the Black Rock's rugged terrain.

Sources at the sheriff's department have revealed that one of the latest to brave the trek is geologist Kerry Dumas. Her supervisor at the Land Bureau in Reno wasn't talking, but our reporters have discovered that Ms Dumas's parents both died in an accident while conducting geological research in the Black Rock twenty-five years ago.

Also setting off into the desert is local deputy sheriff John Eagle. Are these quests personal or professional? And is this sudden interest in one of Nevada's most remote deserts something more than mere coincidence?

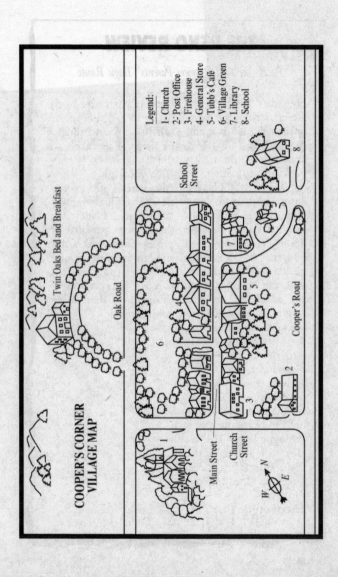

COOPER'S CORNER
VILLAGE MAP

Twin Oaks Bed and Breakfast

Oak Road

Cooper's Road

Main Street

Church Street

School Street

Legend:
1- Church
2- Post Office
3- Firehouse
4- General Store
5- Tubb's Café
6- Village Green
7- Library
8- School

W — N — E — S

COOPER'S CORNER

CJ CARMICHAEL

The Legend

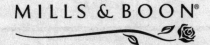

MILLS & BOON®

For helping me with various and sundry research questions my thanks to Dr Gordon Bird, Gord Dunlop, Christine Scheel and Rose Strickland.

As for Jane Porter, thanks could never be enough.
You are a great friend, a valued source of advice and an all-around wonderful person.

Caveat: I have striven for accuracy while writing this book. However, the location of John and Kerry's "treasure" is fictitious. Please do not attempt to find it on your own. You will get lost. And I won't be able to find you.

*First published in Great Britain 2005
by Harlequin Mills & Boon Limited,
Eton House, 18-24 Paradise Road, Richmond, Surrey TW9 1SR*

© Harlequin Books S.A. 2002

CJ Carmichael is acknowledged as the author of this work.

ISBN 0 263 84702 0

142-0905

*Printed and bound in Spain
by Litografia Rosés S.A., Barcelona*

Dear Reader,

What kid doesn't dream of the chance to go on a real treasure hunt? I know I used to, and my daughters, too. For their birthday parties I would draw maps and hide clues to lead them and their friends to hidden treat bags of candies and stickers.

In *The Legend* Kerry Dumas has access to something very few of us ever do—a real map and a real mystery. When she was a child, Kerry's parents perished during a backcountry trek in the high desert of Nevada. No one knows what they were doing miles from civilization, or why such experienced backpackers apparently ran out of water and food. A cryptic map in her father's pocket is the only clue.

When she was eight, Kerry and her best friend, John Eagle, tried to follow that map, to no avail. Now Kerry is all grown up, on the verge of becoming engaged to a man she's worked with for several years. Before making that final commitment, she decides to give the old map one last try.

Who better to help her than her old buddy John? This time she doesn't expect gold and diamonds. She's looking for answers.

To the mysteries of the past…and the future.

I invite you to join Kerry and John in their adventure. One warning—it's summer in the desert. You might want to keep a glass of ice water beside you as you read.

Bon voyage,

CJ Carmichael

PS I'd love to hear from you! Please send mail to the following Canadian address: #1754 - 246 Stewart Green, SW, Calgary, Alberta T3H 3C8, Canada. Or send e-mail to cj@cjcarmichael.com.

THE COOPERS OF COOPER'S CORNER

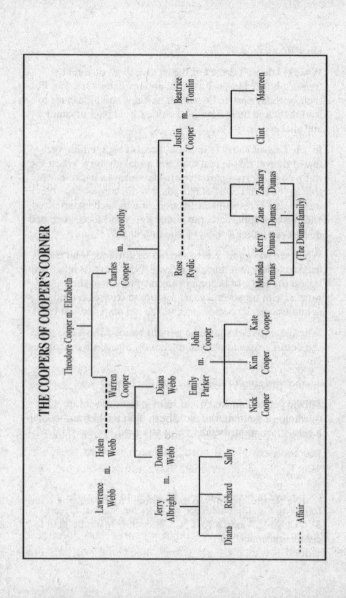

Theodore Cooper m. Elizabeth

Charles Cooper m. Dorothy

Warren Cooper

Lawrence Webb — m. — Helen Webb

Diana Webb

Donna Webb

Jerry Albright — m. — Donna Webb

Diana

Richard

Sally

John Cooper — m. — Emily Parker

Nick Cooper

Kim Cooper

Kate Cooper

Rose Rydic

(The Dumas family)

Melinda Dumas

Kerry Dumas

Zane Dumas

Zachary Dumas

Justin Cooper — m. — Beatrice Tomlin

Clint

Maureen

- - - - - Affair

CHAPTER ONE

THE DUST-COVERED cedar box hadn't been opened in years. Kerry Dumas knelt on the carpet and lifted the old brass latch. Eleanor Dumas—the aunt who had adopted her and raised her from the time she was five—had collected all the treasures of Kerry's childhood in here.

Mementos from those few precious years with her parents, then the time she'd spent on the Dumases' ranch and at school.

Methodically Kerry stacked old report cards, class yearbooks and the photo album her aunt had lovingly compiled for her the year she'd moved out of her poster-plastered bedroom at the ranch for the last time.

Eleanor had made an album for all her kids. The twins—Zach and Zane—and Melinda. Even John had received one. He'd spent so much time at the Twin Bar Ranch, Eleanor must have felt like he was one of her own.

His daddy, Hamilton's foreman, had brought John over every day when he showed up for work and then taken him home every night when he left. John had ridden the elementary school bus along with all the

Dumas brood, shared their after-school snack and the chores, too. Best had been the long summer days, when they'd been able to play for hours, uninterrupted.

After prying apart two of the stiff pages near the front of the album, Kerry paused at an old photo. She and John had been six, maybe seven years old. She was chasing him around the corral, laughing, a lasso in her hand. Presumably they were playing wild horses. It had been one of their favorite games.

She snapped the album closed. She and John weren't close anymore. Hadn't been for years, really, not since she'd come home from college.

Deeper into the box she delved. Here was an envelope containing her baby teeth. Imagine Eleanor saving every one. A clipping from her hair—blond, not yet the rich brown that it was today. And finally, wrapped in plastic, the map her uncle Hamilton had given her on her eighteenth birthday.

Her father's map. Retrieved from the pocket of his trousers at the end of her parents' last, ill-fated foray into the desert.

Their bodies—her mother's and father's—had been located deep within the mountainous region of the Black Rock Desert. Cause of death, her uncle had explained when she was old enough to understand, was dehydration, although there had been evidence of an accident of some sort, too. Her father's left leg had been broken, and he'd suffered some contusions to his head.

The older she became, the more Kerry wondered what her parents had been looking for in that desert. Had they found it before their deaths?

If there were any answers to those questions, this map had to be the key.

She slid the folded sheet from its wrapper. The yellowed paper crackled as she attempted to flatten it on the carpet by her knees. Several blotchy areas of discoloration suggested sweat to Kerry. Or possibly tears? Seeing her father's cryptic pen markings gave her an odd flutter in her stomach, a mixture of excitement and regret.

She'd always been mesmerized by the mysterious markings and notations, especially the drawing at the end of the trail. When she was younger, it had seemed like nothing but a squiggle. Now, as she studied the small sketch with more experienced eyes, she wondered if she only imagined a man's haughty profile.

Although her uncle hadn't given her the map until she turned eighteen, she remembered the first time she'd seen it, much earlier than that.

She and John had been eight. An age when nothing had seemed impossible. At least not to her…

"I'VE GOT a secret," Kerry chanted. Dressed in jeans and an old T-shirt, she jumped on the corral gate. Her transferred momentum sent the old gate swinging inward. The lone horse in the center of the pen eyed the opening with interest.

"You do not." Slowly, Johnny moved to the gap she'd created, his gaze on the unbroken colt.

Kerry wanted him to look at *her*. "I do so, and it's a good one."

"So what is it, then?" With Kerry still perched on the top railing, he swung the gate into the closed position and secured it with a loop of rope.

"I'm not telling."

"That's 'cause you don't have anything to tell."

Kerry knew better than to fall for this. She had three older cousins, after all. "Fine. Then you'll never know about the treasure."

Johnny climbed on the railing next to her. His legs hung down a good two inches farther than hers. She hated that he was taller, that he could run faster, that he was stronger. It was pure delight to tantalize him this way.

"What are you talking about?" he asked.

"I know where a real treasure map is. Hidden in Uncle Hamilton's office." Bringing up her uncle's name was a nice touch. Johnny admired him almost as much as he did his own father.

"I bet."

"It's true."

"Tell me where," he challenged.

"No way." She swung her legs, flushed with her success.

"Why'd you bring up the secret in the first place if you weren't ever going to tell?"

"I thought maybe we could trade secrets. That is,

if you've got one, too…'' She examined the grass stains on the knees of her jeans. They were a really dark green. Aunt Eleanor was going to make her go at them with that slimy bar of laundry soap again.

''I don't have any secrets.''

''Sure you do. I saw you at lunch.'' He'd snuck an extra sandwich and two apples into the pocket of his jacket. There was no reason for him to have done this. Aunt Eleanor let them eat all they wanted. Even between meals, if it wasn't too close to supper.

Johnny's face went so pale she was almost sorry she'd said anything.

''I'll put them back. It wasn't stealing. She said we could have whatever we liked.''

''Of course it wasn't stealing. You can keep them.''

They sat on the railing, Kerry swinging her legs, Johnny still and quiet, for several long moments. The frisky colt dashed around the pen several times, then stopped suddenly and stared despondently toward the pasture and his mother.

Kerry sighed. Having a secret wasn't any fun if the other person wasn't bugging you to let it out. ''When my mom and dad died in the desert, they were following this map. My uncle Hamilton keeps it in his desk. They're going to give it to me when I turn eighteen.''

''Really?''

Kerry held her legs still and nodded. ''Uncle Hamilton thinks Mom and Dad were just doin' some sort of geological survey. *I* know they were searching for treasure. When I grow up, I'm going to find it.''

Johnny continued to stare. ''What kind of treasure?''

Kerry felt a little improvisation was necessary at this point. ''A big chest full of gold and diamonds and stuff.''

''Oh, yeah?'' Johnny stared off in the distance, as if he could see something in the far pasture that she couldn't.

''You can help me go after it if you want. If you're not too scared.''

''Me, scared? You're the one who's too chicken to go on your own.''

''Am not!'' She was, but no way would she admit it. ''Just thought it would be more fun to go together.''

Johnny shrugged. ''Well, maybe…''

He was interested. She could tell. His dark eyes sparkled like polished stones.

''I'll split the treasure with you. Fifty-fifty.'' It was a fair offer—more than fair, since the treasure by rights belonged to her parents.

Johnny's eyes narrowed. ''You sure you're not making this up? I'll bet there isn't really a map.''

''Is so!'' Kerry slid off the fence, landing on her feet in the dirt with a thud. ''Come on and I'll prove it.''

THOSE DAYS with John didn't seem so long ago. And yet, more than twenty years had passed. Kerry sighed.

She knew better than to expect a chest filled with jewels and gold now. All she wanted was to understand what had drawn her parents into the desert. She wanted the truth about what had happened to them and reassurance that their final days had been spent doing something they loved.

Really, she should have made this trip long ago. She couldn't explain why she hadn't. First there was school, then university, then finding that all-important first job. She'd bought a condo, found a guy she was serious about...

But Kerry knew she couldn't procrastinate any longer. Soon she would be getting married and having children. If she didn't make time to check this out now, she never would.

She stowed the cedar chest—minus her parents' map—in her bedroom closet. Just as she slid the door closed, her phone rang.

Knowing it had to be Evan, she considered letting it ring. She didn't have time or energy for another argument.

And yet, this was the man she was planning to marry.

She picked up the receiver from the stand by her bed. "Hello, Evan."

Right away he started in, listing all the reasons she ought to reconsider her plans. "It's not that I don't want you to go. But why by yourself? Desert, mountains, total isolation... It's insane!"

She knew Evan had a point. And she felt guilty— she hadn't been exactly honest with him about this trip she was taking. She'd explained that she wanted to visit the place where her parents had died. But she hadn't told him about the map, afraid he'd scoff at the idea that anything worth finding could be hidden in the harsh high desert of the Black Rock.

"I know my plans seem crazy to you. But this expedition is something I've always wanted to do—like climbing Everest or swimming the English Channel."

Lodging the portable phone between her head and shoulder, Kerry refolded her parents' map and zipped it into the bottom compartment of her backpack. She and Evan had discussed this point just three hours ago at the office. If only he could accept that she wasn't going to change her mind.

"But what, exactly, will you be doing out in that desert for two whole weeks? And why do you need to be alone?"

Again, she had no logical answer. This was something she'd always known she needed to do on her own.

Well, that wasn't the entire truth. There was one person she would have loved to share this trip with. Only one person had ever believed, as she did, that her parents had been on a quest when they died in the desert twenty-five years ago. And only one person knew the Black Rock Desert well enough that he might be able to help her.

But she hadn't even considered asking John to help

her. They barely spoke nowadays. And whenever they attended family gatherings, he seemed to avoid being alone with her.

She supposed John Eagle had outgrown their childhood friendship.

"I don't have a better answer to your question now than I had at work this afternoon. Evan, please, let's stop arguing about this trip."

"But what good will it do to see where your parents died? Kerry, if it's a break you need, why not book a week in a vacation resort in Mexico? And let me come with you. Hell, if you want to avoid the big wedding thing, we could elope while we're at it."

"Evan, I will go to Mexico with you. I might even buy into this eloping thing." She wasn't into dressing up, or big fancy ceremonies, either. "But I have to make this trip first. I have to."

She heard his long sigh. "Honey, you'd make me so happy if you'd just start wearing my ring. You know my parents are planning to fly in from Texas for my birthday next month. It would be the perfect time to make an announcement."

"I *will* wear your ring. As soon as I get back. Plenty of time before your folks arrive, I promise."

She knew that her family was expecting an announcement soon, too. She and Evan had dated for over two years now. Fortunately, everyone in her family seemed to like Evan. Her friends, too.

Except John...

Kerry's gaze fell on a photo that must have fallen

out of that old album. It was the one of her and John playing wild horses. She felt a bittersweet pang for the old, uncomplicated friendship they'd once shared.

So what about John's opinion? It wasn't as if south of Reno he was a big part of her life anymore. He was a deputy sheriff, living in Carson City. Besides, it was entirely possible she'd mistaken his reaction that one time she'd introduced him to Evan at a barbecue out at Zach's ranch.

"I want to take you for dinner the night you get back," Evan said. "Someplace nice."

Kerry took a deep breath. When she got home she'd need a bath and a good night's sleep. But relationships were about compromise, and Evan had been patient. He was trying hard to understand about this trip.

"Dinner. Sure, I'll look forward to it." It was time she put the past behind her and started moving forward with her life. On her last birthday—her thirtieth—she'd realized she was tired of living on her own. She wanted the comfort and security of a husband…and a baby. It seemed the streets and malls of Reno, Nevada, were filled with young mothers and their infants. Soon she wanted to be one of them.

But first she had to get this business of her parents taken care of.

"I really should go, Evan. I still have to pack."

"You'll remember your two-way radio? If you run into trouble, just call, and I'll be there as fast as I can.

You know Will has that charter helicopter company. He owes me a few favors.''

"I'll bring my radio." It irritated her that he would feel the need to remind her. Any fool going into the Black Rock Desert on their own knew enough to bring a radio. She was a fit woman, a geologist with a good job at the Land Bureau. She had plenty of backpacking experience, too, and Evan knew it.

Yet he wasn't the only person in her life with over-protective tendencies. She ought to be used to the treatment by now. Orphaned at five, raised as the youngest of the Dumas children, she'd always been the baby. And her limp didn't help, even though she struggled to conceal it.

Well, this time she was going to prove just how self-reliant she could be.

When Evan finally said goodbye, she checked the time. Almost eight. She ran a key over to the neighbor who lived down the hall and asked her to keep an eye on her place for the next couple of weeks.

"Would you please bring in my mail—go ahead and read the paper, if you'd like. And maybe water my plants if they start to sulk."

"Going on a trip with that nice boyfriend of yours?" Retired schoolteacher Bess Hyatt had just come in from her yoga class. Her gray hair was pulled back in a ponytail, and she had her rubber mat rolled up in her hands.

Kerry gave a noncommittal smile. "I may not be a full two weeks. It depends on the weather." And how well she could read her father's map without getting lost.

"Now, don't worry about your place. I'll keep a close eye on it."

"Thanks, Bess."

That night, Kerry felt like a kid trying to drop off to sleep the night before the first day of school. The next time she slept on this mattress, her trip would be over. Would she have learned anything interesting? Would she be glad she'd gone, or sorry?

CHAPTER TWO

JOHN EAGLE parked his dusty Jeep in his friend's backyard. Blade Silverman and his wife, Karli, had given him permission to leave it here for the duration of his two-week leave from the sheriff's office.

He pulled his long legs from under the steering wheel and stepped down to the hard, caked ground. A cloud of dust rose around his boots.

After checking to make sure he had his knife, then patting the full canteen slung over his shoulders, he ambled to the kitchen door. No one answered his knock, so he dropped his keys inside the screen. Just in case they needed to move his Jeep.

Catching a glimpse of his reflection in the clean window by the sink, he paused. Straight dark hair. Eyes black and round like hunks of polished stone. Once he'd hated the native heritage so distinctively visible in his face. Now he was thankful for it.

He turned his back on the house, on civilization—such as it was in the small town of Gerlach, Nevada—and set out for the high desert on foot.

Here in the northern part of the state, the terrain differed from the sandy dunes and cactus-studded landscape of the south. Sagebrush was the name of the game, and rocks, as well as the ubiquitous mountains. There was water, if you knew where to look for it, and his father had taught him well during their many long treks together.

John wasn't worried about heading out on his own with next to no provisions. He was only attempting what thousands of his ancestors had done before him, when they were much younger than his thirty years.

Spirit quests, they called them, but he was too ingrained in the western way of life to apply the term to his journey. He had his reasons for being here. Reasons that had been made abundantly clear to him last week while sharing a few drinks with his good friend Zach Dumas.

That was when Zach had told him that his cousin Kerry was on the verge of announcing her engagement to Evan Sutcliff. Just hearing Zach pronounce Evan's name was enough to set John's teeth on edge. He'd met the man once and knew he wasn't nearly good enough for Kerry. But Kerry's family seemed to think he was. And so, obviously, did Kerry.

John knew there'd been a subtext to Zach's conversation—*don't wreck this for Kerry.* As if John could. Kerry had never shown the slightest romantic interest in him, and John had always known the Dumas men wouldn't consider him fit for their cousin if she had. Not that he would have considered overstepping his bounds to even try.

Really, from his point of view, the upcoming engagement was a good thing. Finally he'd have to face reality and give up on his foolish juvenile dreams. By the time these two weeks were over, he'd have forgotten all about Kerry Dumas.

That's what this trip was about. He'd had the idea that very night in the bar and had committed himself by telling Zach he was heading out to the desert for a few weeks. He hadn't told Zach why, of course, but maybe Zach had guessed. His old friend had given him a sympathetic look as they'd said their goodbyes.

Did he think John couldn't do it? Get over Kerry?

John knew that he would. What choice did he have?

KERRY AWOKE before her alarm went off the next morning. She felt excited and anxious to get moving. After a quick breakfast, she loaded her car with her gear, then took the interstate east from Reno. The July day was clear, calm and hot—typical summer weather for Nevada. Eventually, she headed north, passing through the Pyramid Lake Paiute Reservation.

At Gerlach, Kerry dropped in at the sheriff's office to let him know of her travel plans. She stopped at the gas station to fill her tank—and a spare jerrican, as well. This would be her last point of contact with amenities of any sort. She went over her checklist one more time to make certain she was fully prepared.

She'd had her Subaru serviced a few days ago. Her pack contained the basics, only: her sleeping bag, clean underwear, a lightweight rain poncho and T-shirts, a small camera and her radio—*got that, Evan?*

Plus she had lots of food. Packages of dehydrated meat and fruit, granola bars, salt tablets and electrolite powder to mix with her water.

She also had all the other essentials. A medical kit, matches, a slender flashlight, a compass.

And the map, of course, still wrapped in plastic to protect it from the sudden heavy rainstorms prevalent this time of year in the mountains.

Filling her lungs with the dry desert air, she slid behind the driver's seat. Heading north on County Road 34, she drove for a few miles before turning at the first playa access point.

Pausing for a moment, she regarded the flat, desolate desert basin known as the Black Rock Desert— one of the largest, flattest places on earth. The ground reminded her of skin under a microscope. Riddled with cracks, it spread before her in an unending plane of nothingness with the mountains, her ultimate destination, a hazy line on the horizon. Packed tread marks fanned out in spiderweb fashion to the western, middle and eastern playas.

She chose western.

Her Subaru lurched forward, sunk slightly into the silt and clay base of the playa, then shot ahead as it gained traction. She was driving on a lake bottom, which sixty thousand years ago had been covered with at least five hundred feet of water. Dust billowed, and she was forced to close her windows. Beneath her hands, Kerry felt the steering wheel jump this way and that as she stuck to the vague trail in front of her.

Her exhilaration at finally starting a journey she'd been planning for most of her life flattened after an hour of boring, straight-ahead driving. The sun bore down on her car as the noon hour approached, giving her air-conditioning a real run for its money.

Outside, the temperature topped a hundred Fahrenheit, she was certain. Inside her vehicle, the warmth was making her head feel fuzzy. Sweat gathered between the car seat and her skin.

More time passed. Her foot took root on the accelerator, and her hands continued playing give-and-take with the steering wheel. The hot air buzzed around her head like a swarm of bloodthirsty insects.

Floating on the heat came the words of a long-ago discussion. One she'd never forgotten, even though at five years of age she'd barely understood it.

"I want to take her along." This was her mother's voice. Kerry was in bed. Or at least she was supposed to be. In truth, she'd wandered down the hall, clutching her flannel blankie and hiding in the shadows.

"I want her to be with us," her mother continued.

"We can't take that risk. It isn't going to be an easy trip. She's practically a baby."

I'm five! I'm a big, big girl! She could ride a horse at her uncle Hamilton's ranch, couldn't she? And she could drive a two-wheeler when all her friends were still on trikes!

Kerry didn't know if she'd imagined that conversation between her parents or if it had really happened. Lately she'd been thinking about them so much. All her life she'd wished they hadn't left her behind on the Dumas ranch. With her childhood sense of invincibility, she'd been certain that if she'd been there, she would have saved them.

Of course, she accepted that if they'd taken her along, in all likelihood she'd have shared their fate.

Jarred from her thoughts, Kerry realized the terrain had begun to change. Hills of brown, parched earth, dotted with sage-green vegetation, rose beyond the northern border of the playa. Farther still, the Black Rock Mountains—her ultimate destination—stood sentry. She gazed at the distant peaks and wondered where, in all that isolation and wilderness, lay her parents' ultimate destination?

Seeing the vast territory before her, the complete lack of civilization, she suffered her first doubt. Could she really do this?

Yes, she could. By taking one step at a time. Rather than worry about her destination, she needed to concentrate on the first leg of her journey. She'd already decided to spend tonight in a cave John had shown her, back when they'd been teenagers.

It had been one of their last escapades together. But she wouldn't mourn their lost friendship now. Instead, she would be grateful that she had a concrete destination in mind, thanks to a conversation she'd had with Zach a few days ago.

She'd been afraid to tell Eleanor and Hamilton the details about her plans—she didn't want to worry them. But she'd realized that someone from her family should know what she was up to. She'd decided to confide in Zach, telling him essentially the same story she'd told Evan.

Unsurprisingly, he'd shared some of the same concerns Evan had.

"The desert is a big place, Kerry. And no gas stations where you can stop to ask directions. Which, being a girl, you'd have no qualms about doing."

"I'll take a map with me." Zach didn't need to know *which* map she'd be using.

"Hmm. Are you sure you don't want company? I could probably work something out if you'd like me to join you."

She'd rolled her eyes. "As if Leslie would let you go for two days, let alone two weeks."

Leslie and Zach were newly in love, and so caught up in each other Kerry sometimes wondered if she and Evan were missing that special spark. But then, she and Evan had known each other much longer than Leslie and Zach.

"Besides," she'd continued, "I'm not totally incapable, you know. I do have backpacking experience. And a radio."

"I wish I could understand why you're so bloody determined to do this. Your parents *died* out there, Kerry."

"Exactly. And I've never seen the place where they spent their last days. Can't you understand, Zach? At five years old I was told my parents were dead. It seemed so unreal at the time. It still does. I guess I'm looking for some kind of closure. You of all people should understand."

Only a few months ago, Zach had been floored to discover that Eleanor and Hamilton weren't his biological parents. The need to find his roots had obsessed him—and put him straight into the path of true love with the doctor who'd discovered the anomaly in the blood records.

Challenged, he'd reluctantly backed down.

"I get it," he'd admitted. "Unanswered questions from the past can be like sand trapped inside your shoes. Eventually you have to stop and shake it out. But you *will* be careful, won't you?"

She'd promised.

"Say, I don't know if John ever showed you, but there's this cave on the southern edge of the mountains that might be a good place to set up camp for a night."

"Good idea." She hadn't thought of that cave in years. "I'll make that my first pit stop."

For some reason Zach had seemed much more comfortable with the idea of her trip once he heard that.

Kerry parked her car and prepared for the second leg of her day's journey—on foot. The sand, fine as dirt, was ground under the soles of her hiking boots as she stepped to the playa floor. At first, the movement of air around her body was a relief. But within seconds, she felt as if someone had covered her face with a hot cloth. She couldn't breathe—

Calm down, Kerry. She forced herself to fill her lungs slowly, then tugged on her hat to protect her ears from sunburn as she went to the back of her car to get her gear.

The sun was blinding as she took off her sunglasses to apply sunscreen and lip balm. She had on long sleeves and thin pants, but made sure to cover the back of her neck and her hands before capping the tube and slipping it into one of the small compartments of her backpack. Then she hoisted the pack— all thirty pounds of it—onto her back.

This was it, then. Everything she'd need for the next week or two had better be in here.

Or she would be in big trouble.

JOHN EAGLE could hear voices in the wind. He hadn't always been able to do this. But now, standing on a rocky outcrop in an area so remote there was no sign of man's supposed domination over the earth, he could hear the singing of his ancestors.

They reminded him that he was no more significant than a grain of sand in the desert around him. That his problems were nothing in the overall scheme of life.

Let go of her, John Eagle, the voices said. He was sure of it. *Let go of everything, all that's in the past, and start fresh.* But in the next second, there were no voices, just wind. The strong, incessant airflow that usually preceded a desert rainstorm.

John narrowed his eyes and focused on the gath-

ering clouds. Like dust from an advancing herd of
buffalo, the sand and water particles billowed from
the great Sierra Nevadas on the western horizon.

Ten minutes, fifteen? He wasn't as good at pre-
dicting these storms as his father was or his grandfather had been. For too long he'd been embarrassed
about his native heritage instead of embracing it.
Even now, his interest and belief were halfhearted at
best. Except for moments like these, when he felt
something primitive stir his blood. A connection to
the land and to his people that couldn't be denied.

A connection? John shook his head. More likely
the imaginings of a lonely, bitter man. Wind was just
moving air, after all, air that was already getting heav-
ier, damper. Fifteen minutes earlier, he'd seen some
scrub jays flitting between the piñon pines, alerted by
the changing weather patterns.

A downpour in the desert was never a pleasant experience. The rain came in deluges the baked earth
couldn't absorb fast enough. The thing to do was gain
a little elevation in case of flash flooding in the flat
playas and canyon floors. He was already high
enough, but John was interested in staying warm and
dry.

So he headed for his cave. He'd thought of it that
way, possessively, ever since he'd found it when he
was out hiking with his father around age ten or
eleven. It was his special place, marked with his
childhood charcoal etchings and filled with all sorts

of desert trophies, including an almost complete coyote skeleton.

It had given Kerry quite a start, the time he'd brought her here with him. He hadn't shared the place with many people, only two or three. Now, as he dipped his head to gain passageway, he was sorry Kerry had been one of them.

He'd come here to exorcise her from his heart, but it was all too easy to imagine her sitting across from his tiny fire. Or to hear her laugh echoing off the stone walls.

John crumbled dead sagebrush onto the embers, which still smoked from breakfast. He added a couple of sticks of dried wood, then went to stand at the mouth of the cave.

He'd only been here a few days and already he wondered if he wasn't going a little strange in the head. His thoughts kept turning to the vision quests of his ancestors. Although John didn't believe in the possibility of communing with the spiritual world, he didn't completely disbelieve, either.

He knew that to his ancestors, visions were considered important gifts from the beyond. They offered wisdom that, if interpreted properly, could improve life for the people who lived so vulnerably off the land.

His grandfather's visions had earned him the place of a powerful spiritual shaman among his people. Bunk, John would have said even five years ago, before he'd taken the time to listen to the old man. He had more respect now, though. He knew his grandfather had possessed a special gift. One that defied scientific explanation.

On his deathbed, John's grandfather had astounded John by telling him that this gift wouldn't die with him.

"You have it too, my son. I've seen the signs."

Much as he'd come to love the old shaman, John had refused to take those last words seriously. He hadn't even thought of them much until now.

But wouldn't it be perfect if a dream could solve all his problems? Tell him what to do about Kerry, how to get over her once and for all?

They'd been best friends growing up. They'd gone to school together, traveled on the same bus and played together at recess and on the ranch, too. Then, in junior high, Kerry had transferred to private school, thanks to the wishes of her parents and the trust fund they'd left for her.

He'd never forget the way he'd felt, watching her grow up from the sidelines. Each time she came home from that fancy school, then later from college, it seemed she'd become a little more beautiful, a little more poised.

A little more distant.

He'd lost her even before she'd fallen in love with this Evan Sutcliff—a geologist who worked with Kerry at the Land Bureau.

Thinking of Sutcliff, John felt a tightening in his chest, a black anger in his heart. His reaction frightened him. He took pride in his self-control. His father had raised him never to strike out in anger. Between them, they'd had reason enough to deplore physical violence.

Yet, for the first time in his life, John felt the sort of thunderous impulses that led men—and women—to commit heinous acts. He had to conquer these feelings, had to accept Kerry's choice. His self-respect and the honor of his family depended on him rising above his weakness.

Outside, the keening wind abated. John not only heard the silence, he felt the absence of motion down to his bones. He drew in a deep breath, then another. Waiting. Waiting.

And finally the storm hit. Water thrashed from the skies, turning the world into one gray blur. The noise of water slapping against rock drowned out all other sounds, and yet, as the wind had done earlier, the deluge seemed to be carrying a message to him.

Kerry, Kerry, Kerry. Her name pounded against his eardrums, assaulting his senses as persistently as the pungent smoke from his fire.

Gripping the stick he held in his hand, John went to sit by the fire. He jabbed at the burning wood, then closed his eyes as a thick cloud of smoke wafted in front of his face. He coughed, then opened his eyes, blinking in the dull light.

There she was. Standing at the cave opening. Her form silhouetted against the gray of the rain. Her hair soaking, her body covered in a clear plastic poncho.

Kerry Dumas.

Was he having a vision, after all?

CHAPTER THREE

THE OPENING in the rock was barely visible through the curtain of falling water. Kerry pushed her wet bangs off her forehead and stumbled forward.

She'd been caught in desert rainstorms before, but surely this was the worst. Her plastic poncho hung uselessly around her drenched body. She felt like she was carrying an extra twenty pounds of water in her clothing and hair. The stuff sluiced down her neck, over her face, into her eyes. She could barely see.

But this was the cave John had taken her to that long-ago magical summer afternoon. They'd driven in his father's four by four, then hiked for five hours. A hot, grueling climb, but worth every ounce of their sweat.

Kerry scrambled on the slick limestone surface, slid, recovered her balance. Just a few more feet.

As she drew closer, she sniffed. Was that smoke in the air? She rubbed more water from her eyes and went on. At the entrance she paused, then tentatively peered inside.

Through the cave's solemn darkness danced a faint golden glow. Someone was here, all right, sitting cross-legged on the ground next to a blazing campfire.

A man. A very primitive-looking man.

He was bare-chested, and his skin glowed like amber in the fire's light, his face eerily distorted by flickering shadows. She saw that he stared at her without seeming to really see her. His extreme stillness along with his expression made her wonder if he might be in some sort of trance.

Trepidation bordering on fear kept her pinned to the entrance, just far enough under cover to protect herself from the worst of the rain.

God, he was massive. His smooth brown skin displayed a powerfully developed chest and long, muscular arms. With his dark hair, thick and wild, he seemed more dangerous than any creature she'd ever seen. She cleared her throat.

"Hello?"

He didn't blink. Didn't adjust the grim, uncompromising set of his mouth, either.

"I'm sorry if I'm disturbing you. But the rain—" She waved a hand to indicate the storm even as she wondered if she might be safer out there than in here.

When the man stood, she thought about running. Then told herself she was being ridiculous. Where could she go that this man couldn't catch her if he wanted?

He was closer to seven feet than six, without a trace of fat to mar the beautiful, sculpted lines of his body. Her already thrumming heart rate accelerated.

Again she thought of escape. The cave offered few opportunities for hide-and-seek. It was wider than it was deep and only about twenty feet by eight. On the wall beyond the fire, she could see the charcoal drawings John had made the day they'd eaten their lunch here.

The man made his first step toward her. With the fire at his back, his face became lost in shadow. Kerry swallowed and raised her chin.

"Would you mind if I shared this cave with you—just until the rain stops?"

He paused, tilted his head a fraction to her left. "Kerry?"

It took her a second to recall the familiar voice, no longer spoken at a boy's pitch.

"John, is that you?" Why hadn't she recognized him right away despite the tricky lighting? Because now she knew, without a doubt, that this man was John.

Part of the reason was his body—his magnificent, primal body. She was used to him in street clothes. And his hair—it must have grown several inches. She'd had no idea it was this thick.

"John?" she asked again.

After several more seconds, he nodded. "What are you doing here, Kerry?"

Moving with the sleek purposefulness of a cougar and a hunter's watchful, cautious eyes, he came up to her. She swallowed away a new and different fear. Not of a stranger, but of a friend who might not be what he appeared.

After all, how well did she know John Eagle now?

Over the years he'd become more and more distant, to the point where she would hesitate before giving him a phone call.

To make matters worse, he didn't seem pleased to see her. Not in the least.

A crazy shiver of fear made her stumble as she took a step backward.

He steadied her with a quick hand to her arm. ''Are you all right?''

Kerry blinked aside her ridiculous unease. Close up, he was John. Simply John. She knew his face as well as that of any other member of her family.

''I'm fine.'' She attempted a smile, which he didn't return. Carefully she assessed his proud, earth-toned features, trying to pin down the exact change in him. Same chiseled cheekbones, sharp and high. Straight nose with just a hint of a hook at the bridge. Well-defined mouth, usually curling with amusement.

Why was he so somber? Had she interrupted something important?

''I'm sorry if I'm intruding.''

''You were caught by the rain.'' He repeated what she'd said earlier. ''But what are you doing here?''

His fingers tightened. He couldn't know he was frightening her. Why had she never before noticed how utterly black his eyes were? She stared and stared but couldn't find the bottom of them.

So busy was she studying him, she was hardly aware that he regarded her with a similar intensity. He shook his head. ''You're real.''

He uttered the words so softly she barely heard them and certainly didn't understand what he meant. Of course she was real. She felt her body start to tremble, and with it, her words.

"John—" She tried to say *Johnny,* but the familiar name wouldn't come. "I'm sorry if I startled you, but please knock it off with this staring routine. It's freaking me out." She truly was scared. There was something so intense about the way he was looking at her. Like a sorcerer casting a dark, evil spell.

Finally his face softened. "Kerry, only you could get yourself into a predicament like this one." He dropped the viselike grip on her shoulder and gave her a friendly, one-armed hug. "You're freezing. Come on, let's get closer to the fire."

With that, everything became okay. She'd been suffering from an overactive imagination, she told herself, fueled by the darkness of the cave and the remoteness of the location.

Breath, stored in her lungs like a last reserve of water, whooshed out in a gush. "For a few seconds there, I didn't recognize you."

He slid her pack from her shoulders and propped it against the wall, then removed her useless poncho. "I see this did a good job of keeping you dry."

Acknowledging her soaked clothing with a shrug, she sank next to him by the fire and watched as he added a few pieces of wood.

"I've taken a couple of weeks off work to go back-packing in the mountains. I drove from Reno to Gerlach this morning, then started across the playa. I left my car at approximately the same place we did that day you took me up here." She glanced around the cave walls again. Hard to believe fourteen years had passed since then.

"Why are you by yourself?"

She shrugged.

"What about your...fiancé?" John's voice was low and steady. Still, that pause made her check his eyes to see if they'd tell her anything his words had omitted.

But she couldn't read a thing in his calm, contained expression.

"We're not officially engaged yet." She held out her hands to the fire, trying to imagine Evan's solitaire diamond sparkling on the fourth finger of her left hand. "Isn't the desert a crazy place. You boil all day, then freeze all night. This fire is glorious."

John frowned. She was about to ask what she'd done wrong. The next thing she knew, he was reaching behind her. He gathered her shoulder-length hair into a cord and squeezed. Water streamed to the rock floor. "You're soaking. From head—"

"To toe," she agreed, wiggling her clammy feet. She really ought to get out of her wet boots and socks.

She'd no sooner had the thought than John was tugging at her laces.

"I can do it myself, thanks." She pushed his hands away but was dismayed to find that, drenched as they were, the knots weren't very cooperative.

"I wonder how often I've heard you say those very words."

He was laughing at her, and she felt a childish resentment. "Don't you get all superior on me," she warned. "We're the exact same age, remember."

"Nope. I'm a week older."

He was taunting her, as he'd done when they were children. Finally, she worked a fingernail between the strands of her laces and loosened the knot. Her boot came off with a disgusting slurping sound.

Ignoring her self-consciousness, she pulled at her sock. The thick cotton dripped water. Ugh.

Briskly, John reached over and took care of the second boot and sock. As he worked, she noticed four marks on the back of his left hand, like pinpricks in a row. He'd had them forever. She remembered thinking, when she was a kid, that they were some sort of strange birthmark.

Now she realized they looked more like scars.

She sneaked another look at his face. His features were guarded and still as he spread the socks over a rock by the fire and propped her boots beside them.

"Do you have a change of clothes?" He eyed her soaked cotton pants and top.

"A T-shirt and some underwear."

John nodded at her pack. "Fix yourself up, then crawl into your sleeping bag to keep warm. If we lay out your trousers now, they'll dry by morning."

His plan made sense. Her drenched pants and shirt were extremely uncomfortable. So why was she reluctant to comply? Because she felt self-conscious? But this was her childhood friend.

"Fine. Turn to the wall a minute."

He didn't respond, and as their gazes locked yet again, she was uneasily aware that while John may have seemed like family, in actual fact, he wasn't. John was a guy and she was a female. And this sizzling in the air between them had nothing to do with his little campfire.

Abruptly John turned his head, and she told herself she was being silly. Briskly, she unstrapped her sleeping bag from her pack and peeled off the waterproof cover. She slipped out of her clothes, hesitating when she came to her damp panties and bra.

What the hell. Off with them, too. Quickly, she spread everything close to the fire then scrambled into clean undies and a thin-strapped tank top before curling into her sleeping bag. All the while, she kept watch on John. He didn't move a muscle or speak a word. Perhaps he'd fallen asleep sitting up.

But with perfect timing, he turned the instant she was safely covered.

"That's better," he said. "Now let me see your parents' map."

"What?"

He'd guessed. But how? Last time they'd seen the map they'd been children. Neither of them had mentioned it in years.

"Don't give me that blank look, Kerry Dumas.

Why else would you be out in the Black Rock on your own?''

She sighed. What was the point of trying to keep it secret? Anyway, John might be able to give her some pointers. Hadn't she thought earlier that he was the one person who might be of some help?

She nodded toward her pack. ''Bottom zipper compartment.''

John pulled out the plastic-wrapped package.

She was still suspicious about how quickly he'd figured her out. And the coincidence of finding him here in the first place. ''Zach didn't tell you my plans, did he?''

If he had, she'd make sure she was wearing steel-toed boots the next time she saw her older cousin.

''Zach knew you were coming out here?''

She nodded.

He raised his eyebrows. ''Interesting. But no, he didn't say anything. Although I did speak to him about *my* plans. If he had mentioned that you were coming out to the desert on your own, I would've told him he was crazy to let you go.''

''He wasn't keen on the idea. But I am an adult.'' Why was she forever needing to remind people of this fact?

''Yeah, Kerry. You're an adult. Still, it's never smart to go out in the high desert on your own.''

''Oh, so you have someone with you, then?'' She pretended to scan the cave for another person.

John gave her an exasperated smirk for an answer.

"You can't mean to tell me you're here all alone?" She mocked him, even as her indignation grew. "But then, you're a big strong man, right? You're capable of surviving in the desert all by yourself.

"Well, I've got news for you. So am I!"

John shook his head. "I know you're capable, Kerry. That's not what I meant."

Yeah, right.

"I'm just wondering why Sutcliff didn't insist on coming with you."

"Of course Evan volunteered to come with me," she snapped. "But this is something I imagined doing on my own." *Or else with you.* But she couldn't admit that to John. Not now. "I've never showed that map to anyone, John. Or even talked about it." She knew others would be skeptical, might even laugh.

"But you've got to admit you'd have an easier time with a partner. Especially one who knew his way around this country."

Was he speaking about Evan? Or himself? "I've had plenty of experience in the backcountry. And I can read a map."

"Yes, but how accurate is it? Your father's hand-drawn sketch...it probably isn't even to scale."

John was all too right on that point. Her father had been a geologist, not a cartographer. And from what she'd been told, he'd sketched the map from one helicopter trip over the terrain. Up close, the landmarks would be much different from the way they appeared in the air.

John's gaze flicked to hers. "I know this country, Kerry. I've spent a lot of time here with my father."

"That's true." She met his gaze for several long moments, certain he was about to volunteer his services. She was almost disappointed when he changed the subject.

"So, do you have a route mapped out for tomorrow?"

"Um, sort of."

"Show me." He tapped the map.

John's cave wasn't marked on her father's map. She had only a cursory idea where they were at this moment. But no need for John to know that. "Later. I've had a long day and I'm hungry. How about we have a little dinner first?"

She noticed John didn't seem to have brought any provisions for himself. At least nothing she could see. Her sight had adjusted somewhat to the dim lighting, and she'd had a chance to case the place. Beyond his clutter of artifacts, including lots of disgusting animal bones, there was only a makeshift bed a few feet from where she was sitting.

"I'll get you something from your pack," John offered.

"Take enough for yourself, as well. I brought lots."

Rummaging through her supplies, he grunted. "You don't have to feed me. I'll catch something in the morning."

"Don't be stubborn, John. You can see I have plenty of food. And I won't touch a bite of it if you don't."

WELL, KERRY WAS as stubborn as ever. John wished he could find the trait annoying. Instead, he admired it.

He'd always loved her spirit, her courage, her willingness to put her whole heart into everything she did. He couldn't believe she was here in his cave—it couldn't be coincidence.

So was it fate? Or had Zach conspired to bring them together? He thought of their conversation in the bar, the warning about Kerry's upcoming engagement, and knew that couldn't be it.

"Here." He passed Kerry a stick of beef jerky. She poked a bare arm from the sleeping bag, her smooth tanned shoulder gleaming. Already her hair had started to dry, and lay like cashmere against her skin.

If this was fate at work, then what a cruel fate it was. He needed to forget about Kerry Dumas. He'd come here to plan his future without her. Now he was faced with her company in the intimate confines of this cave, in the midst of a desolate wilderness.

That she was close to naked inside that sleeping bag—her cotton briefs and bra on bold display in front of him—was the final, ironic twist to the entire setup.

"You have some, too, John."

"Fine." He helped himself to a stick of the jerky. "I was going to brew tea. Want a cup?"

"Please."

Kerry had the basic supplies in her pack, but he chose to use his own. Over the years he'd been coming here, he'd collected a variety of cooking implements, including a concave stone he used for boiling water. Into this he placed some of the herbs he'd gathered that morning.

"Those look interesting. Nothing narcotic, I hope," Kerry said, watching him.

For the first time in days, John felt amused. "As if I would dare pull a stunt like that with a woman who wouldn't even touch a cigarette."

She remembered right away and made a face at him. "They were vile-smelling."

He had to laugh. She'd been twelve, and it had been a dare, and he knew it had killed her to back down. He'd found the half-empty package buried in some straw while they were cleaning stalls, fallen from the pocket of a ranch hand, probably.

When the tea was ready, he poured steaming liquid into makeshift cups and passed her one. Again, he was favored with a view of feminine shoulder, the sharp line of her collarbone, the hint of swelling lower down.

"It's hot," he warned. "Be careful."

She raised her eyebrows at him. "Yeah. Boiling liquids are like that."

It had been so long since they'd been alone together. He'd forgotten how much she hated protective behavior. As the youngest in the Dumas clan, she probably still garnered plenty of it from her family. And from just about every eligible male she met.

Kerry was tall and fit, but her delicate facial structure made her seem fragile, and no amount of grime or tough talk, or even ability, could overcome that impression. Add the limp, a congenital defect she refused to acknowledge, and what was a man to do?

All his life John had wanted to look out for her. And she'd fought him every time he tried.

So why should it be any different now?

"Okay, we've eaten. Now let's look at the map." He bent over the stained yellow document. And remembered…

Last time he'd seen this, he'd been eight. Kerry had been certain she'd found the yellow brick road to a treasure trove of riches. And he'd been satisfied just to have a dream to hold on to. If only for a little while.

Over the years, he'd thought about the map and wondered. But by the time he and Kerry were old enough to make an honest effort of the job, Kerry was in private school, and they hardly saw each other. And when she came home for the holidays, each time he was blown away by the changes in her. The emerging woman had excited him, but frightened him, too.

He knew who he was and who she was and that there were certain fantasies that could never come true. He was more likely to find a carved chest full of gold and diamonds than he was to have Kerry as his woman. He'd known this truth all along—and so he'd hidden his feelings. But fool that he was, he hadn't stopped dreaming.

Not about treasure.

Or about the girl.

"Where are we right now?" Kerry hopped over in her sleeping bag for a closer view of the map.

"Here." He pressed his smallest finger to the spot. "On the edge of the big mountains. We could pick up your father's trail just a little farther on, by this river here." He pointed again.

Kerry regarded him thoughtfully. "We?"

"I meant you," he said smoothly.

Her eyes still held a measure of suspicion as she shifted her attention to the map. "I figure it'll take me three days, maybe four, one way."

"That's optimistic." He'd been following the trail in his mind, trying to relate her father's markings to the land he'd explored with his father. "Some portions of this map are pretty vague."

"Yeah," she agreed. But she didn't seem worried.

He wished he could be so confident. "See this squiggle?"

Kerry leaned over his pointed finger, squinting to make out the pale ink marking in the dim light.

"That's a solid rock face," he said. "My grandfather told me stories about a secret passageway, but I've never seen it."

She studied the map. "But there has to be a way through. There's no other route to that valley."

"Exactly." Her father had named the destination

of his map Black Valley. In the center was the drawing John remembered puzzling over as a kid. He picked up the yellowed paper and studied it. "This looks like a man's profile."

"I thought so, too!" Kerry ran her finger over the wavy line. "See his forehead, his nose…all very strong features."

"Like a native American," John said softly.

"Yes."

She added nothing, as if afraid she'd offended him. In the past he'd been very touchy about his heritage. But the rough sketch had triggered a memory of one of his grandfather's stories, told just a few months before the old man passed away.

"There's a legend of my grandfather's… This profile reminds me of it."

"Yes?" In her excitement, Kerry let the sleeping bag drop from her shoulders. Even in the pale firelight, it was obvious she wore no bra under her thin cotton tank top.

Intense longing stabbed John, an unexpected jolt of physical reality. He felt stunned, derailed, couldn't remember what they'd been talking about.

Kerry, of course, had no idea what she'd done to him. She didn't seem to notice his momentary lapse of concentration.

"Tell me more, John," she said, her eyes washed with excitement. "I'd love to hear your grandfather's legend."

CHAPTER FOUR

KERRY HAD ALWAYS considered John's native heritage fascinating, but she knew he hadn't felt the same way growing up. When the kids in their grade school teased him about living in a teepee and running naked around campfires, he'd withdrawn into a furious silence.

Privately, he'd confessed that he hated being different. As far as he was concerned, he was no more native American than any of the Dumas children who'd grown up at the ranch. Back then he'd tried to dress the same, talk the same and eat the same as the other kids. Looking at him now, though, Kerry realized there could be no doubt about his true heritage. With his bare chest, jet-black hair and cross-legged posture, he was a living picture of the heritage he'd fought to deny.

"The legend goes back to the beginning of time," John began. "Before the desert, when forests grew in this land and game was plentiful."

Entranced by his singsong voice, Kerry closed her eyes. The words sounded like the beginning to a fairy tale, but she was a geologist and knew better. One had only to look as far as the last ice age to find evidence that this alkaline, parched land had once been a verdant Eden.

"Into this time a boy was born. And although he wasn't a chief's son, the wise men of the tribe said he would make his mark on the land."

A chill shimmied down her spine. John's voice had altered slightly, and with her eyes shut, she could almost imagine she was listening to his grandfather— even though she'd only met the man once.

"The boy grew into such a strong, fearless brave that even the mountain lions cowered in his presence."

When John paused to ease his dry throat with a sip of tea, Kerry opened her eyes and sighed. "Yes, go on…"

He leaned over his cupped hands. With the light from the fire exaggerating his bone structure and setting off the gleaming blackness of his hair and eyes, he was once again the thrilling stranger she'd first thought him to be.

She felt a faint ripple of the unease she'd experienced in those initial moments of entering the cave. There were many layers to John Eagle. She wondered if she'd ever known him as well as she thought.

"One night, an enormous explosion erupted in the heavens and showered sparks into the air. The earth shook and caught on fire. Trees and plants burned. Panicked animals fled in all directions."

Kerry pictured the mayhem, imagined the horror.

"The people of the tribe ran for their lives. All

except the brave. He refused to leave. Not even in the face of certain death. When the fire finally dissipated, a few of the other braves returned to look for him, but all that remained was the outline of his face, burned forever into the rock.''

''The outline of his face,'' she repeated slowly. Picking up the map carefully, she studied the drawing again. No wonder John had thought of this legend when he'd seen it.

''What if it isn't just a story?'' she mused. ''What if it really happened?''

''I don't think the legend is meant to be interpreted literally.''

''I know.'' But still, she imagined possibilities. A volcano? A terrible rock slide? Forest fire? ''Whatever disaster the natives might have experienced at that time could have something to do with what my parents were searching for. After all, as geologists, facts like these would be very interesting to them.''

''Well, since you're a geologist, too, I suppose you would know. To me it's a story. And that's it.''

John gave her a dark, brooding look she couldn't begin to analyze. He finished his tea, then unfolded his legs and went to the cave's entrance. ''The rain has stopped.''

Suddenly aware of the silence outside, Kerry nodded. ''It's so still, isn't it? That's what I always notice when I'm in the desert. Nowhere else is there such a complete, utter lack of sound.''

''It's getting late. You should sleep. Dawn comes

early in the summer, and we need to take advantage
of the cooler morning temperatures for traveling.''

We? He'd used the wrong pronoun for the second
time that night. But she was too tired to spark another
argument. She'd deal with John in the morning. Exhaustion had crept up on her. Suddenly she couldn't
keep her eyes open.

''Night, John,'' she said, curling into her covers.

Last night, Kerry had lain awake for hours, too excited to sleep. Tonight she fell asleep seconds after
John put the fire out. Her last thought was that he
would look really good in a loincloth. Perhaps she
would put forward the suggestion the next day.

MORNING BROUGHT warmth and light and the distant
sound of birds. Before Kerry opened her eyes, she
knew John had been up for hours. He'd been out
hunting and had caught something, which was roasting on the open fire. The scent made the practical
provisions in her knapsack seem unappetizing.

Opening her eyes, she saw that he'd put on his shirt
and washed his hair, slicking it back from his face.
Those changes, plus the brilliant morning sunshine,
made her wonder how she could possibly not have
recognized him last night.

She must have been more freaked out by that storm
than she'd thought.

Stretching out her legs, she expected to feel the soft
comfort of her sleeping bag. Instead, her skin scraped

against the hard rock floor. Sometime in the night, she must have undone the zipper.

She glanced at John and realized he'd been looking at her legs. Hmm. That was strange. As far as she'd been able to tell, John only took note of the fact that she was a woman when he was trying to explain why she couldn't do something.

"So do they pass inspection?" She stood and began to roll up her sleeping bag.

"What?"

"My legs. I saw you checking them out."

His eyes narrowed, then he shrugged. "I thought I saw a spider, is all."

"Oh, really?" No, she'd recognized that gleam in his eye, but she decided to let it drop. "Something smells good."

He turned to the fire and prodded the coals. Skewered on a roughly fashioned spit above the low-burning embers was his catch. The unidentifiable creature was about the size of a small game hen, a little shriveled from cooking, but glistening with a toasty almond-colored glaze that boggled her morning-challenged brain.

"Let me guess. Julia Child dropped in and I missed her."

John basted the meat with a thick liquid he'd concocted in the same bowl he'd used for tea the previous night. "What are you talking about? I'm just roasting a—"

"Don't tell me!" She figured she'd be happier not

knowing. John wasn't above cooking a rattler if he had to. Happily, this skewered creature was much too plump to be that. Yawning, she looked for her clothes, which were no longer stretched out in front of the fire.

John had made a neat pile of them beside her backpack. On top were her panties, neatly folded in half. She glanced from the stacked clothing to him and was annoyed to see him holding back a smirk.

"What's so funny?"

"White cotton granny briefs?" He raised his eyebrows.

"Cotton is comfortable." She shot the words back. "But it's not *all* I own."

"Really?"

"Oh, shut up!" She tossed a small stone toward his feet. "Now turn around so I can get dressed. White cotton briefs and all."

"I don't see why I should bother. You pretty much displayed all a man could be interested in while you were sleeping."

Oh, no…

John laughed at her expression. "Don't worry. It was mostly just arms and legs."

Mostly?

"Okay, I'll clear out and let you dress in peace. I'm going to fill my canteen. May as well top up yours while I'm at it."

"Thanks." She waited until he left the cave, then grabbed her clothes. The pants were stiff and wrinkled and not very clean, but at least they were dry. As she smoothed the cotton with her hands, she wondered about the tone in John's voice. And in hers. Definite sexual nuances that until now had been conspicuously absent in their relationship.

Her friendship with John had never had anything to do with sex. They were pals. He treated her like one of the guys.

Truthfully, until last night, she'd never noticed what a hunky-looking guy he was. Well, of course she'd noticed. But she hadn't *noticed*. Not in a way that made her heart race and her stomach twist in a most confusing manner.

When he returned with the water, she was tying the laces on her boots.

"Ready?" He nodded approvingly. "We'll eat and then get moving. I figure we can clock about four hours before it gets too hot to travel."

There it was again. "John, why do you keep saying 'we'? You know I'm doing this on my own."

"I know that was your plan. But since I'm here anyway, why not let me tag along?"

"You don't want to tag along. You want to baby-sit me. And frankly, I find that rather insulting."

"Kerry—you don't have a clue how to read that map."

"I'll figure it out. Besides, John, you must have had your own reasons for being here. I don't want to wreck your plans."

"I just had some extra weeks of vacation coming

to me at the sheriff's office. Didn't have any place else to go, so I headed here.'' His tone was too smooth. A sure sign he was hiding something.

But prying secrets from John had never been easy. Kerry glanced around the cave, speculating. He'd brought precious little with him. Just his clothes and canteen and a knife he kept strapped to his ankle. Not much else.

There had to be a reason he'd made this trip so difficult for himself. He was too Western, and too old, for this to be on one of those coming-of-age endurance tests she knew were part of many North American native cultures.

But she couldn't think of any other explanation.

She didn't know much about what was expected on a real spirit quest. But she suspected that visits from friends, sharing beef jerky sticks and reading old treasure maps probably weren't on the approved activity list.

"I've spoiled things for you."

"Nothing's spoiled, Kerry. Except maybe this meat if you don't hurry up and eat your share.'' He removed the cooked game from the spit and divided it into two portions. "Here. This'll beat that dried stuff you had last night."

But she didn't care about food at the moment. "I don't *need* your help, John. You've seen my backpack. You know I'm prepared."

"Forget it, Kerry. I'm not leaving you out here on your own. What if you fell and broke your leg?"

Which was what had happened to her father.

"I have a radio."

He dismissed that point with a scowl. "You always did have a problem admitting when you need help."

"Excuse me?"

"How about the time you fell off your horse because you wouldn't ask about the cinch on the new saddle? Or the night you stalled my truck on the highway because you refused to admit you'd never driven a standard before? Or the—"

"Stop! The thing with your truck happened more than ten years ago. It's not fair to drag up all those old stories." Especially when he had so many of them. "Anyway, I'm not stubborn. I'm determined."

He picked up his plate and sat next to her. "And I admire you for it. But there comes a time when it's smart to accept a helping hand."

She sighed, unsure how she'd ended up arguing against something that she found quite appealing.

"Come on, Kerry. Eat. You'll be sorry later if you don't."

Kerry nibbled on her meat. The glaze was sweet and absolutely delicious. "I had no idea you were such a good cook." Wasn't that something she should know about the person who'd been her best friend for most of her life?

"It's a newly acquired skill."

Well, that explained it. These days, the only times she saw John were on the ranch or at Eleanor and Hamilton's town house.

And yet as children, they'd been inseparable. Back then, she never would have dreamed of going on a trip like this without Johnny.

"I DON'T THINK your uncle Hamilton would want us in his office."

Johnny was a daredevil about some things. He'd jump on a sheep's back if you promised him a quarter and he was never afraid when a panicked horse started running toward him. But when it came to breaking rules—especially those set by Eleanor and Hamilton—he could be a real stickler.

"Come on, Johnny. The map used to belong to my parents. That means it's mine now." Her uncle had no right to hide it away from her. He should've told her about it. Why did everyone treat her like such a baby?

Kerry eased the heavy pine door closed and checked out the familiar room. Her uncle's sanctuary smelled of warm straw and horses, despite Aunt Eleanor's rule about washing up before coming into the house. Kerry walked past the bookshelves and the two leather chairs cozied up next to it, heading straight for the heavy wooden desk by the window.

"My father says it's wrong to disturb a man's privacy." Johnny hung back at the door, his hands on the knob, obviously ready to turn and run at a moment's notice.

But he wouldn't take off without her, Kerry knew. In the years she'd been living on the ranch with the

Dumases, Johnny had never backed out on her, not even when she was doing something he'd told her not to do.

"What about *my* privacy? That letter belongs to me!" She pulled on the dull silver handle of the middle drawer. It wouldn't budge. She pulled harder, and it gave with a loud racket.

"Quiet!"

Aunt Eleanor was hanging laundry on the line, but who knew when she'd be back?

"Sorry." Kerry shuffled through pens and paper but quickly saw that the map wasn't there. She moved to the series of drawers that ran down the right-hand side of the desk. She had to search all the way to the bottom before she saw the familiar-looking bundle.

"This is it!" She grabbed the plastic bag, which contained a carefully folded rectangular sheet. Other items were nestled beside the map in the drawer, including a small, fuzzy blue box and a couple of watches she immediately recognized.

Her parents'.

She stared at the jewelry with horrid fascination. Someone must've taken them from the dead bodies. She couldn't bear to think about that.

"Okay," she told Johnny. "We can go now."

"Make sure you shut the drawer."

"Oh, yeah." She pressed her shoe against it until the edges were flush with the rest of the desk. There. Once she and Johnny found the treasure, they'd put the map back, and her uncle would never know he'd been raided.

Safely out of the house with the map, the two of them headed behind the big stable. Even in the shade the temperature was hot. The dust in the air made Kerry's nose itch.

"Let's see the map." Johnny held out his hand.

"Hey. It's my map." She fingered the plastic-coated package.

"Okay then. Open it up, will you?" Johnny had been against her plan in the first place, but he sure was eager now.

"Wait a minute." Kerry hadn't known what to expect. But as she unfolded the sheet of delicate paper, she knew her parents hadn't let her down. Hand drawn in black ink—except for one red marking—the map couldn't have looked more mysterious. Johnny crouched next to her.

"Wow! It does look like a treasure map, all right. Look at that!"

Kerry felt very proud of her parents then. The paper was old and kind of wrinkly, and the black markings were very mysterious. "Where's the X?" she wondered.

"I don't think there is an X. But the treasure must be here." Johnny pointed to a strange drawing at the end of the wavering ink trail. "And over here is where the trail starts."

He pointed again, and Kerry tried to make sense of the meandering lincs and all the little markings. The triangles were mountains, obviously. The wiggly lines maybe rivers or creeks.

"Oh, gosh!" This was too exciting! Kerry couldn't wait to dig up the old chest and find out what was inside. "Let's start now!"

Johnny looked at her scornfully. "We have to make plans. Get organized. Pack."

Yeah, packing was a good idea. "What do we need? Pajamas and a toothbrush?"

"Pajamas? A toothbrush?" Johnny sounded so scornful she knew she'd made a mistake.

"How about matches?" she added quickly. "And maybe a flashlight, too?"

"And water. And a knife."

Kerry shivered. "A knife?"

"We've got to be prepared for anything."

Well, there were rattlers in the mountains. And scorpions. "Okay, a knife, too. I can get all this from the house. It should only take a few minutes."

"Kerry, we can't leave on this trip from here."

"Why not?"

Johnny shook the map at her. "Because it doesn't start at your ranch. Look at all these mountains. And these dots are the desert."

Kerry studied the old markings. It was easy to see where the trail began on paper. But where was that in real life?

"There's desert and mountain by my place," Johnny volunteered.

What a relief. She should have known Johnny would know what to do. "How do we get there?"

"*We* don't. *I* do. I'll leave tonight, after Dad's in bed."

"Without me?"

"You can't walk to my house. It's too far," he told her.

"That's not fair! It's my map! Ask your dad if I can come for a sleepover."

"That's a dumb idea."

"Why is it a dumb idea? You've had sleepovers here." Not often, but occasionally, when his dad had to go on overnight trips with her uncle.

"I'm just not allowed to have sleepovers, okay?" Johnny's face looked the way it did when the kids at school teased him, and that made Kerry feel all weird in her stomach.

"Don't be mad, Johnny."

"I'm not. But you can't come to my house. Don't worry. I'll share the treasure with you when I get back."

He held out a hand. Did he expect her to pass him the map? Did he really think she was going to let him go on this treasure hunt by himself?

But what choice did she have? She couldn't get to the mountains by herself. Unless...

Hmm. She could think of one way. It was so simple, she was tempted to brag to Johnny. But what if he tried to talk her out of it?

"Here's the map." She slapped it into his hands,

pretending to be annoyed. "Just remember we're partners. Fifty-fifty."

"Fifty-fifty," Johnny agreed.

"FINISHED eating, Kerry? We should get moving." John snuffed out their fire, then doused it with dry sand.

Kerry finished the last of her breakfast, then bent for her pack. John beat her to it. Heaving the nylon bag off the ground, he went to settle it on his shoulders.

"John, you can come if you insist. But I'm carrying my own pack."

"But I have nothing to carry. Why not let me—"

"You've already had your way at least once today. Now it's my turn."

With reluctance, he turned and let her slide the pack off his shoulders and onto her own.

"It's too heavy." He fussed like an old grandmother.

"Only thirty pounds or so." She'd traveled with more weight, but had packed lightly out of respect for the summer heat and the difficult terrain. Tightening the straps at her waist, she glanced at him.

"Ready?"

"Damn right, I am. We're going to do it this time, Kerry." He grinned at her. "And we might even have a little fun while we're at it."

She felt a bubbling enthusiasm, thinking, hoping he might be right. "Okay then, let's get moving."

For a moment they paused at the mouth of the cave, looking into the mountains they'd be traversing that day. For all the beauty of the arching mountains and the shimmering sky, the view inspired both awe and respect.

Kerry felt, more than put words to, a prayer for their safety.

At her side, John touched her elbow. ''One more thing, Kerry, before we get started.''

She wondered what they could possibly have forgotten.

''When we find the treasure, don't forget, we share it fifty-fifty.''

She knew he was teasing her. But still she echoed his word like a solemn vow. ''Fifty-fifty.''

And they were off.

CHAPTER FIVE

IF KERRY'S PRESENCE on this mountain with him had been meant as some sort of test, John knew he was already failing. Ten minutes into their first stretch of hiking, he was focused more on Kerry than on the trail they were climbing.

He couldn't stop thinking about how she'd looked that morning, half in, half out of her unzipped sleeping bag, cheeks flushed, hair mussed.

Ignore her, he'd cautioned himself. But since that was an impossibility, he'd decided to leave the cave and hunt for breakfast.

Ahead of him by two strides, Kerry stopped abruptly to adjust the straps on her pack.

"Changed your mind about me carrying that for you?"

She shot that idea down with a dirty look.

He held out his hands in surrender. Offering to help had been a mistake, but the instinct was too ingrained in him to do otherwise. Kerry had always brought out his protective instincts. And as a deputy sheriff, he had a lot of them.

"We need to avoid those lower elevations," he reminded her, when she started to veer toward a lower grade. "The river is still swollen from last night's rain. At least we had plenty of water to fill our canteens. I'm afraid finding water won't be so easy later on."

Striding around an outcropping of rock, John felt the bright sunlight hit his back. Kerry bumped into his side as she came into the light, too. "Wow, it's already so hot."

For a moment he stared into the denim blue of her eyes, then she shielded them with sunglasses. She brushed a hand over her unkempt hair, pulled it back and fastened it securely with an elastic, then put on her hat.

She looked so cute, he was tempted to tap a finger to the end of her nose. Balling up his hand instead, he reminded himself that she was out of bounds.

She was the rancher's cosseted niece. He'd been the son of the hired hand.

And she was engaged, or pretty damn near engaged. To a man who seemed to have no problem with letting her wander alone in the desert. Now, that didn't make sense. In Evan's shoes, John would definitely have insisted on going with Kerry. What kind of man was this Sutcliff?

Ahead of him, Kerry set a moderate pace despite her bad foot and the uneven terrain. John was so used to her slight limp he didn't notice it. She never drew attention to her disability. In all the years he'd known her, she rarely complained, even though he knew from Eleanor that she was often in pain by the end of the day.

Kerry rounded a quick turn in the path and glanced back. "Not going too fast for you, am I?"

He loved her cheekiness. "Pace yourself, Queen Kerry. We'll be gaining elevation most of the day."

She scowled at the nickname. All the years she was growing up, Kerry had never been a girlie girl. She'd skipped the phase of wanting to dress up and have tea parties. He couldn't remember ever seeing her play with a doll.

Ironic that Kerry the tomboy had turned out to be such a pretty woman. With her lovely, delicate features, she'd look great in a dress, but he'd rarely seen her in one. Even for work Kerry favored a casual, sporty look. He was glad she had never been one to dress to please others, to primp with makeup or fuss with the style of her hair. Her lack of artifice was one of the greatest things about her.

He lengthened his stride for a few moments to catch up to her.

"Beautiful out here, isn't it?" he said. After the rain, the struggling desert plants were tinged with green. The clear blue sky provided perfect relief to the dark, rocky angles of the mountains. Even the air, though hot, had a cleaner, fresher tang today.

"Yes. And so still, too. I haven't seen as much as a bird. It's almost spooky. How did you manage to catch our breakfast?"

"I was up earlier," he reminded her. "It's too hot

now. Any creature with common sense is hiding out in the shade.''

''I hope that includes snakes and scorpions.''

''In this heat they'll be holed up in small rock crevices or taking shelter under the pines.'' He knew Kerry wasn't frightened of the creatures themselves, just their poisonous venom. When they were kids...

''Remember our reptile zoo?'' Kerry put a hand on his arm.

''Funny. That's just what I was thinking about.'' At its peak, they'd had about five snakes and several varieties of lizards—none of them poisonous. Not that they hadn't tried, but Eleanor wouldn't allow it. They'd built cages out of scraps from around the ranch and exhausted themselves catching enough insects and mice to keep the reptiles fed. ''I remember you insisted we name them after the minerals in your rock collection.''

''That's right. There was Obsidian and Jasper— remember the collared lizards?''

She kept her hand on his arm as they were talking. He was sure the touch, the connection between them meant nothing to her. But his heart hammered, his blood surged. She probably didn't realize what she was doing. For sure she had no idea what she was doing to *him*.

She never had. That was one of the reasons being with her had become such hard work. It took so much energy to make certain he never betrayed his desire with an inappropriate look or touch.

She let her arm drop to her side. As if on a switch, his body cooled down.

"We were quite the pair, weren't we?" Kerry was still talking about the past.

"You came up with all the ideas. I provided the brawn."

"Really? Whose idea was it to climb up on the barn roof? We lost our riding privileges for a week that time, if I remember right."

"Oh, yeah." Maybe the ideas hadn't all originated with her. Still, she *had* come up with some pretty zany projects. But there'd been quiet times, too. Like the hot summer afternoons when they'd sprawled on the lawn under the big shade trees next to the house and talked about any old thing that popped into their heads.

She would play with her hair sometimes, unwinding the braids her aunt put in every morning. Slowly she'd curl the strands around her fingers, sometimes chewing on the ends.

He'd longed to touch her hair. It seemed so soft compared with his. Softer than anything he'd ever seen, and clean and shiny. He supposed that was the beginning of his obsession with her, even though he'd been too young to know what was happening at the time.

"I used to tell you everything back then," she said.

"I know." He'd loved being the one she trusted. And if he hadn't been quite as open in return, he didn't think she'd noticed. Certainly, he'd shared

more of his thoughts and feelings with her than anyone else. But he'd had some secrets too ugly for a
little girl's ears, even if she was a rough, tough tomboy.

Kerry sighed. "Too bad life has to get so complicated. There are days when I'd do anything to be able
to step back in time. Don't you think we had the most
idyllic childhood on the Twin Bar?"

On the ranch, sure. Trouble was, while Kerry lived
there twenty-four hours a day, he'd had to go home
at night when his father finished working.

"What happened, John? When did things change
between us?" She tilted her head in his direction, her
expression wistful.

Oh, God, Kerry, let's not go there. "I'm not sure
what you mean."

She frowned. "You always knew what I was thinking without me saying a word."

He still did. Like right now. He knew she was nos-
talgic for her old childhood friend, for their former
warm, accepting, happy relationship. A platonic relationship that had gone the way of orange Popsicles
and bicycle bells.

For her smile, he'd do almost anything. But it was
physically impossible for him to be the boy he'd once
been, to turn back the clock, to recapture what they'd
shared.

"We're still friends, aren't we?" he asked.

"Yes... But..."

She stumbled, as she sometimes did when she was

tired or not concentrating. He caught her by the elbow and was surprised when she didn't shake him off with her usual stubborn independence.

"I guess things change when you grow up," she said, returning to their conversation.

She definitely had. Each time she'd come home from that damn private school of hers, he'd felt he was meeting somebody new. It was only natural that she grew taller and developed high, firm breasts, that her hips began to flare and her lips took on a womanly fullness.

To be fair, even though her body was changing, she'd never acted any different. In her heart she remained the friendly, curious girl who loved horses and rocks and her best friend, Johnny.

He was the one who'd pushed her away, unable to reconcile his new feelings and desires with their old easy camaraderie. During those years when she was away, he'd grown into a man, and she'd become his dream woman. It wasn't just a friend he wanted anymore when she jumped out of the passenger seat of her uncle Hamilton's truck on her summer and Christmas breaks. It was a lover.

Sometimes he'd felt he wouldn't be able to keep breathing if he couldn't have her. Other times he'd just been angry. At her, at himself, at their situation.

So he'd pulled back—he'd had to—a little more each time. He'd become extra cautious around her, careful not to look at her too long or to touch her unnecessarily. And he'd watched what he said, as well, so she wouldn't guess just how much he missed her when she was gone or how much time he spent thinking about her in ways that would have shocked her if she'd known.

"John?" She shook his arm. "You don't understand anything I'm saying, do you?"

He couldn't let her know what he really thought. What he really felt. So he shrugged and gave her a blank look.

Obviously disappointed with his response, she grimaced and shook her head. "You men. You're so oblivious."

KERRY HAD grown up with her cousins, Zach and Zane, so she knew how obtuse men could be about emotional issues. But how could John not be aware of the fundamental changes in their friendship?

Maybe he knew but he just didn't care. She stared into his deep black eyes and tightened her grip on his forearm, wishing she could guess what thoughts lay beneath his calm, still expression. Close as they'd been, she'd never had the ability to read John the way he was so capable of doing with her.

"You say we're friends, John, but are we?" She felt as she had those first few minutes in the cave last night, as if she were dealing with a stranger, and a potentially dangerous one at that. Just because she'd known the boy didn't necessarily mean she knew the man.

"Do you trust me?" he asked.

She went with her first instinct, her gut reaction, even though her senses were in turmoil. "Yes."

"Then we're friends."

As if it could be that simple.

She realized she was still touching his arm and had been this whole while. With awareness came a new focus. His muscles were hard, his skin warm and smooth. She'd reached out to him without thinking, but now she was hit by a wave of heat she wasn't used to feeling around John.

A man-woman kind of heat. What was happening to her?

She dropped her hand.

"You look hot. Better drink some water," John suggested. "You have to be careful not to get dehydrated."

She knew then that her cheeks were flaming, and she was glad to have the desert sun to blame. Locating the straw to her canteen, she pulled in several mouthfuls of refreshing liquid, then set out walking again.

Her footsteps seemed to draw more energy from her now. She distracted herself from the weight of her pack, her bad leg and the off-putting conversation with John by thinking of Evan. She thought about the idea of elopement versus a big wedding with all her family.

Truthfully, she didn't care which route they took. All she wanted was a family and children of her own. Melinda was so lucky. Did she have any idea how

Kerry envied her two darling children? And Zach with his twin boys from his first marriage.

"What was that big sigh about?"

She glanced sideways at her stranger-friend and wondered about his love life.

She knew John had had girlfriends, but she'd never met any of them, even though she would have liked to. Pressing Zach and Zane for details had netted very little useful information. Zach's only comment was that John had impeccable taste when it came to brunettes.

"Do you think you'll ever get married, John?"

"Don't think about it much."

She couldn't accept that answer. "Come on. You turned thirty this year, too. That had to start you thinking about the future."

"Is that what it did for you?"

"Oh, yeah. Big time." Thirty had seemed to come out of nowhere. Maybe that was because she was the youngest in the Dumas family, accustomed to being viewed as the baby. Turning thirty had been a shock and a bit of a wake-up call, as well.

"The biological clock started ticking, is that it?"

"In part, yes." She wanted babies. That was definitely part of it. "Turning thirty forced me to see myself as a grown-up. I suppose that sounds strange, given that I've been living and working on my own for almost ten years." She leaned a hand against the rock face to her right and shortened her stride as the trail steepened.

"I get what you mean."

Of course he did. For a moment she felt a flash of joy—the pure pleasure of being with someone who understood and who cared. It was a feeling she'd always associated with John, only this time, tangled with it, were other, more complicated emotions.

Sorrow, regret, a touch of longing... Trying to dissect her feelings only made her feel worse. Why did everything have to be so complicated?

And why had she never noticed the pattern of their conversations before? She saw one clearly now. She initiated confidences, shared her deepest dreams and fears, while John listened and understood but rarely reciprocated.

"Don't you want kids?" This time, John would talk. She wouldn't let him off so easily anymore.

He took a few strides in silence. "I don't think it's my destiny to be a father."

What a cop-out! "Since when do you believe in destiny?"

"Maybe I used the wrong word. All I'm saying is that there are things you learn to accept in life."

"And..." *God, could this trail get any steeper?* "You think not having children is something you'll have to accept?" She couldn't understand why he would have reached this conclusion. She'd seen him with Melinda's young ones and Zach's boys and knew he enjoyed kids.

Kerry fought for oxygen as she climbed the steep

stretch. A flat rock slab beckoned, and she leaned against it for a break and to enjoy the view.

Turning, she gazed over the territory they'd covered. In the distance were the vast stretches of the Black Rock Desert. The air above the playa seemed to shimmer as the sun's heat radiated off the dark earth.

Before she knew what was happening, John had lifted her onto the rock perch, then jumped up to sit beside her. The ledge was high enough that her feet dangled in the air, reminding her of the many times the two of them had balanced on the wooden corral gate and watched her uncle and John's father work with the young horses.

Remembering those days gave her a peaceful, happy feeling. She'd been so lucky to have a friend like John. And until now, she hadn't realized how much she'd missed him. Maybe they could recapture some of that old magic during the next few days. Maybe she could get him to think of her as his old pal Kerry again.

But was that what she really wanted?

She shifted her weight on the rock, and suddenly her arm was pressed against John's. The heat gathering in the spot where her skin pressed against his— separated only by the thinnest of cotton—became all she could focus on.

Was this new physical awareness something only she was experiencing? She shot a sideways glance at John but could tell nothing from his profile.

For the first time, she wondered what John's male impressions of her were. Did he find her attractive? Sexy? Had he ever felt the urge…

Kerry swatted at a horsefly as it swooped by her head.

She found *him* attractive and sexy. Perhaps she was foolish for being surprised by the realization. John had been tall for his age, and too thin, but he'd been an eye-catching kid all the same. Not that she'd ever dared to tell him that his dark coloring and sharp-boned features gave him exotic good looks bordering on true beauty.

And now that he'd developed the muscles to match his height, he was handsome enough to be dangerous.

There it was again. That word she never would have associated with her childhood friend before, but now just couldn't get out of her head. It was silly, wasn't it? John wasn't dangerous.

The stupid horsefly returned, this time buzzing around her sweaty neck. John brushed his hand over her cotton T-shirt, frightening it away.

''Thanks,'' she said. ''I hate those things.''

''I remember.''

His hand touched lightly at the base of her neck, then brushed past her ponytail. Subtly, he shifted so that not even their shoulders were in contact anymore. Kerry swung her legs and wondered why she wished he'd kept his hand where it was.

''John?''

He looked at her, waiting for the rest of her words.

His face bore a patient expression she'd seen many times before. John never rushed and rarely interrupted. He was used to her untangling her thoughts with her words like this.

"Do you ever wonder what it would be like…. I mean, have you ever felt the urge to—?" She stopped, afraid there were limits to what you could ask someone you'd grown up with. If she admitted this sudden attraction, she'd be putting him on the spot. Honesty would force him to confess he considered her like a sister. Of course, that would be good. She didn't want their relationship to change, other than to return to the way it used to be. As comfortable as worn denim and as warm as a mug of cocoa on a winter night.

No. That wasn't what she'd wanted, at all. Not a minute ago. Not even right now. She wanted him to kiss her. Oh, my God, she wanted him to kiss her.

"KERRY… What were you saying?" John saw the confusion in her face and wondered if she'd felt that flash of sexual awareness passing between them. Or was he crazy to think that he could have the same chaotic effect on her senses as she had on his?

"Just babbling, as usual." She slid off the rock and landed solidly on her feet.

John jumped down, too, blocking her from the path. "I've never considered you the babbling kind. Kerry, anything you said was always worth listening to."

She took another drink of water, maybe just to distance herself from him. Wiping the moisture from her lips with the back of her hand gave her a few precious moments to dissemble.

"Have you ever come close to asking a woman to marry you?" she asked.

He stared, blinked, then laughed. "Kerry, that is *not* what you were about to say earlier."

"Maybe not. But have you?" She started walking again, and he followed. Her shirt clung to her body, damp from sweat. He was glad her hat and sunglasses shielded her head and face from the scorching rays.

"No, I never have. Never even come close."

"But do you want to get married?"

"What's with all the questions today?"

"We don't have much else to do. Besides, when we talk, I forget about how bloody hot it is out here."

John paused, assessing her inner reserves. As if aware that she was being judged, she increased her pace slightly, smiled and said, "Not that I'm tired or anything."

She'd never admit it, even if she was. Well, he would force the issue in another hour or so, but for now he thought they were probably safe to continue.

"I don't know about getting married," he said. "But it sounds like you do...what with your upcoming engagement." He hated turning the conversation in this direction, but he did so purposefully, wanting to cause himself pain, to remember that this woman was off-limits. Something a moment of sexual attraction—imagined or not—could never change.

"Yes. Do you remember Evan, John? You met him once at one of Zach's barbecues."

He sure had. And hadn't even bothered to try and assess the man impartially. Any guy who was interested in Kerry was automatically his enemy.

"Well?" she pressed. "What did you think of him? You weren't very friendly, as I recall."

"It doesn't matter what I think. You obviously love the guy."

"Evan's a great person. He can be very sweet."

Was it just him, or was her answer a little lame? "You met at the Land Bureau, right?" he probed, not sure why it was necessary to torture himself with the details. Only that there was more to Kerry's questions than she was letting on.

"Yes. Evan used to work for an oil company in Dallas before he took the position with the Land Bureau in Reno. His parents still live in Texas."

"Have you met them?"

"No, but I will shortly. They're coming for a holiday soon. Evan wants to announce our engagement while they're here."

"I guess that makes sense."

"I guess…"

His heart lifted at the uncertainty in her voice. Now he knew what this conversation was about. "But you're not sure you want to marry him, are you?"

"No, no, that's not it," she said hurriedly. "I know

Evan will make a good husband and father. Sometimes I wonder if I'm good enough for him.''

"Bull. That's not what you wonder, at all.''

She stopped, and he almost marched right into her.
He put out his arms, and she turned into them. With
his hands on her shoulders, they glared at each other.

"You're right,'' she conceded suddenly. "I am
scared. I always thought that when you met the person
you were supposed to marry, you would just know he
was the one. But even though Evan and I have dated
for a long time, I don't have that feeling.''

He knew it was wrong, but her words brought him
an intense joy.

"But I'm probably being simplistic and idealistic,
right?'' Kerry went on. "I mean, in the real world,
people just try to make the best decision they can. I'd
say Evan and I have a good chance of making a happy
marriage. We're both geologists and we both love the
outdoors.''

"It's important to have similar interests.'' He had
to agree. It didn't take a genius to see Kerry wanted
him to validate her choice of Sutcliff for her husband.

Was that the right thing for him to do, then? But
John didn't think it was envy that made him believe
Kerry could do better than Evan Sutcliff.

"Do you think it's possible to ever be a hundred
percent certain that you've met the right person to
share your life with?''

Be careful, John cautioned himself. "Tough call,

Kerry. Maybe you should ask someone with a little more experience on the subject.''

''Yeah?''

She sounded disappointed with him. While she paused for a sip of water, he checked the position of the sun and mentally adjusted the plans he'd made that morning. They were traveling slower than he'd expected—not that he'd ever tell Kerry. She'd only start pushing harder and run the risk of overexerting herself.

Still, the nearest source of water he knew about was an hour away at this rate. Should they keep moving through the heat to make it? Or rest for a few hours, then try again later?

''Feel like a break?'' he asked.

Kerry paused to mop the sheen of sweat from her forehead. ''This isn't the stopping place we agreed on.''

''No, but we aren't on a guided tour. We can be flexible.'' He kept his tone light, careful to conceal his concern. Her face was flushed, and her breathing was still elevated, even though they'd paused for over a minute. Was he pushing too hard?

No. She'd been setting the pace all the way. But then no one needed to push Kerry. She did a damned fine job of it on her own.

He wasn't surprised when she shook her head. ''Let's keep going. If we break early now, we won't make the mileage we planned for the day.''

She started again, leaving him no alternative but to

trail along. He wondered if she'd bring up Evan once more, but she didn't. For twenty minutes they marched in silence.

As they gained elevation, the path narrowed. To their right rose the hard rock wall of the mountain. To the left the ground sloped off sharply, a maze of boulders and sparse vegetation. Here, even the piñon pines struggled for survival. They grew in twisted, tormented shapes, the desert's gothic creations.

Scrambling over the rock-strewn ground was second nature to John, but Kerry had to slow her pace. Worried, John followed as closely as he dared.

"Watch your step."

"Stop fussing." She turned to toss the comment his way, and that was her mistake. In an instant, she lost her balance. Loose rock scattered down the path toward him. Exposed from what had probably seemed like a secure hiding spot, an eight-inch scorpion scurried in first one direction, then another.

Kerry screamed. More rock crumbled and fell. John rushed to catch her, but he was too late. Although Kerry tried to throw her weight to the right and the relative safety of the mountain face, gravity pulled her left. She tumbled off the path, down the steeply pitched slope.

CHAPTER SIX

"KERRY!"

She heard John call her name as her legs buckled traitorously beneath her. Off balance, she teetered, then hit the earth with a painful crunch and began rolling down the slope of the mountain.

Shielding her head with her arms, she felt the rocks tear at her skin through her clothes. The prickly branch of a piñon caught at her shirt, only to snap and release its hold a second later. On she rolled like a heap of dried sagebrush, until finally she hit the side of a boulder secure enough to hold her weight. For the first few seconds she lay there, too stunned to react.

Then John called out again.

"Kerry? Oh, my God, Kerry!"

She heard him scramble down the slope, his boots scraping against the rock and dirt. Every square inch of her body hurt, ached; she was scared to open her eyes and survey the extent of her injuries. At least she was conscious. Even that much seemed a miracle.

How could she have been so clumsy? John would be convinced she was an idiot, a total incompetent who could never survive in the desert alone.

She struggled to raise her head from the ground, but the sight of her clothing made her cringe. Her pants were torn in several places. Blood was already tingeing the sand-colored fabric red.

"Kerry, are you okay?" John picked his way slowly along the unstable rocky slope.

"I think so." She eased into a sitting position.

"Dizzy? Seeing double?"

"No. My head aches a little, but that's all."

"Tell me what day it is."

"I can't remember." The calendar was always a blur when she wasn't at work. "I know I was at the office on Friday and drove to Gerlach on Saturday." She'd parked her car and walked to his cave that night. "That must make today Sunday."

"Right. Good for you!" John smiled in relief as he finally reached her. He ran a hand over her head. His tender touch made her feel cared for and...loved. Until she realized he was only checking for bumps and abrasions.

"I think your legs took the worst of it. Can you move them? I hope to God nothing's broken."

Now was the time to find out. Both legs hurt like hell, but she was able to straighten them without much trouble. "Not one of my more graceful maneuvers, was it?"

"You fell, Kerry. It could happen to anyone."

Not to him. She blinked several times, fighting a sudden need to cry. She hurt, but not that much. So why this weepy sensation?

John ran his hands lightly over her limbs. "I can't believe it, but it looks like you're getting out of this with a few abrasions and probably some pretty awful bruises. You were smart to protect your head. A hard knock against one of those rocks could've given you a bad concussion."

He took a deep breath; she could hear it rattling in his chest.

"We're never going to make our target now," she realized.

"To hell with the target." He held out a hand, and she grasped it. Then he bent to put his other arm around her waist. Carefully, he eased her into a standing position.

"Okay?"

She nodded.

He unclasped the straps of her backpack. "This probably saved your back from some nasty gashes." He transferred the load to his shoulders. "You're trembling."

"I know." But it wasn't because of her injuries. It was *him,* first holding her so intimately, then putting his hands to the buckles that rested on her upper chest and waist. She was reminded of the moment when they'd been sitting on that rock. She hadn't imagined the feeling; she knew that now. The man-woman thing was back in full force. And why not? They may have grown up together, but they weren't related.

What about Evan?

She couldn't think about him right now.

"Want me to carry you up the hill?"

"I'm fine, John. I can make it on my own."

"Maybe you should rest a few more minutes."

No, they'd already lost too much time. She broke away and began picking her way toward the path. Even though she moved slowly and chose her footholds carefully, her body protested.

After an exasperated sigh, John followed, so close she could hear the huff of his breath. If she lost her balance, she'd tumble right into him. That was probably the point, from his perspective.

But she wasn't going to lose her balance. Not again. Kerry tested every foothold as she scrambled up the rock-strewn slope. The sun was definitely her enemy now. The suffocating heat aggravated her pounding head, and her sweaty palms made it difficult to get a good grip on the rocks.

She was close to the breaking point, she recognized. Pure determination kept her moving when she longed to sink to the ground and close her eyes.

Eventually, she reached the path, with John still right behind her.

"Let's find some shelter from the sun."

She didn't have the strength to argue. John led her to a level area under a stone outcrop that acted like an awning.

"We can rest here." He slipped off her pack and unrolled her sleeping bag. "Try and catch a little sleep. When the sun is lower, we can make up the time we've lost."

"Okay." She'd have agreed to anything at this point. Gratefully, she collapsed onto the spread-out bedding.

"Not so fast," John said. "I know you're tired, but we have to clean those cuts of yours. Infection spreads fast in the desert." He rummaged through her pack to find her first-aid kit.

"Bottom compartment, left-hand side." God, this was such a pain, but no question he was right. Unfortunately, most of the abrasions were on her legs and arms. The only way to get at them, to make sure nothing was missed...

"You want me to take my clothes off?"

The question hung in the air between them for several seconds. She could have sworn John almost smiled. But his tone was no-nonsense when he finally answered.

"You see any alternative?"

"I guess not. But this is becoming a habit. Tell you what. Don't bother to turn around this time. It's not like you've never seen me in a bikini before." She wiggled out of her pants, then pulled her shirt over her head. Actually, it felt wonderful to rid her skin of the garments.

"Ah, Kerry." John shook his head at the sight of all the scrapes and cuts. "I hope you have enough bandages in here."

They ended up using almost the entire supply and half the tube of antiseptic ointment. John gave her two pain-relief tablets, making sure she washed them down with plenty of water.

Finally, she was able to lower her head to the sleeping bag and relax. It was hot even in the shade, so she felt no compulsion to put her clothes on. Still, John would probably think it was strange if she didn't....

She fell asleep contemplating the dilemma. When she awoke, John had something roasting for their dinner. He'd dug a fire pit several yards away, surrounded it by rocks, then fashioned a spit from a long, straight branch that must have been difficult to find, given how twisted all the trees here were.

"You haven't slept at all, have you?"

"I wasn't tired. How do you feel now?"

"Better." It was then that she remembered she was dressed in her bra and panties. She pulled on her shirt, then reached for her pants and found them damp. He'd washed out the bloodstains.

For some bizarre reason, this made her want to cry again. She turned her back to him on the vague pretext of modesty, then stepped into her pants. John was taking such good care of her. And she'd shown precious little appreciation.

Taking a deep breath, she stepped from under the rocky overhang and checked the sky. The sun shimmered from the west. "Thanks for everything, John. Looks like I was out of it for several hours."

"You needed the rest."

The air had cooled a good twenty degrees. She

went to stand by his fire, watching as he gave a half-turn to the sizzling meat. John hadn't been a hunter when he was younger. This had to be a skill he'd learned from his father or perhaps his grandfather.

Funny how well he knew her family, while his—except for his father—were all but strangers to her. She'd only met his grandfather once, and his mother never.

This was part of the enigma that was John, she realized. On one level she knew him well. But there were many layers she'd never glimpsed. Mostly because he wouldn't let her.

"You know what I've been thinking about?" she asked.

"Air-conditioning and lemonade with ice?"

"Oh, Lord. Don't even go there." She pictured a glass the way her aunt made it. Tangy and ice-cold in a mug frosted from the freezer...

Wait a minute. He was changing the subject again, and she hadn't even started.

"I was thinking about *you,* John. And all the things I don't know about you."

"I'm a pretty simple guy. Not that interesting."

John, simple? At one time she'd believed that, believed they were as close as two friends could be. But she'd been very, very wrong.

"You know, when I first saw you in the cave, I thought you were a stranger. A trick of lighting, I guess, and the way you were dressed." Or, rather, half undressed. "Then later, after I'd recognized you,

I felt an enormous relief. It's John. It's my good friend, John.''

He didn't say anything. But he was listening. Muscles tensed, eyes wary. Yes, he was paying attention, all right.

"Only *not* my good friend. At least, not anymore. And maybe not ever. I shared my secrets, John, but you never shared yours.'' Did she sound like a petulant eight-year-old? But she couldn't hold her feelings back any longer.

"I'm sorry you see it that way, Kerry. Maybe I kept my feelings to myself a lot. But that's the way I was raised, the way I am.''

"You kept more than your feelings from me. In all the years we knew each other, I was never once invited to your house.''

Her aunt and uncle made a point of including John and his father in all the big Dumas family dinners and holidays. Often, they'd come. But always just the two of them. "Do you realize I never even met your mother?''

John's shoulders slumped as he dropped his gaze to the fire. "She didn't socialize much.''

Kerry knew she'd dived into dangerous waters by mentioning his mother. She'd heard the rumors. The older kids at school had said Mrs. Eagle was crazy. Kerry had asked her aunt, and Eleanor had explained that John's mother had health problems. *It's a sad situation, and those children are very cruel to tease.*

"Yes, but we were like family, weren't we?''

Kerry couldn't let the subject drop. Not this time. "With all those invitations to our house, you'd think just once your mother—"

"She was a drunk, okay?" John jerked his head up and hurled the words at her.

Kerry shut her mouth.

"She was a fat, stinking, disgusting drunk. That's why she never came to any of your family's turkey dinners or attended school concerts or picked me up before the school bus came to take me to my dentist appointment. That's why you never met my mother."

He turned his back to her, and Kerry wanted to sink into the earth. She'd finally done it. Jabbed at John hard enough to unearth one of his secrets.

"I'm sorry."

He gave no sign he even heard the apology.

"I was an idiot. I shouldn't have made you talk about something so painful."

She saw his shoulders rise, then fall, on a deep breath.

"It's okay, Kerry. I'm thirty years old. You'd think I'd have gotten over it by now." He turned toward her.

"You want to know the ironic thing about my mother? According to my father, she was once the prettiest girl in the area, a real happy person who loved having a good time. But all that changed after she ran off to become Mrs. Eagle. Her entire community rejected not only her new husband, but her, as well. And the half-breed son who came around seven months later? He was nothing but an embarrassment to the family.''

Kerry wanted to deny the story. Such blatant prejudice didn't happen. Not in this day and age. But remembering the teasing John had endured at school, she knew it did.

''My mother coped with her problems by drinking. Eventually she lost her figure and her good looks. She spent her days crying into the mirror or the bottle. So you see, I couldn't invite my friends over to play because I couldn't be sure my mother wouldn't puke on the floor, right in front of them.''

Kerry felt awful. John hadn't fit in anywhere. Not with his mother's family, not with the kids at school. And he'd rejected his father's heritage, at least in those days. He must have felt terribly isolated.

''Don't look so miserable, Kerry. It wasn't that bad. I had my father. And the Dumases. Besides, those days are over. Now I'm considered a respectable member of society.''

Was that why he'd gone into law enforcement? To become someone people could look up to and trust? She bet it was. Suddenly she was very proud of the man he had become.

''I wish I had done more to help you.''

''Like what? Come on, you were a kid.''

''I could have been a better friend.'' She'd assumed the Dumases' warm blanket of love and acceptance had enveloped him, too, never guessing just how outside the fold he really felt.

"I didn't even make your mother's funeral," she recalled with sadness. Just three months ago, she'd gone to the funeral of a colleague's mother. And yet she hadn't extended the same courtesy to her best friend. "I should have been there for you."

"You were away at school."

She remembered her aunt phoning with the news—it had been her senior year, two weeks before finals. For the first time she'd struggled over her weekly letter to John. He'd never spoken about his mother, so she had little idea how to comfort him. She'd ended up penning a line or two of standard condolences. So sorry about your loss, that sort of thing. When John had scribbled a note back—he generally wrote about one letter to her four—he'd made no mention at all of the event. It was as though it hadn't really happened.

Now she wanted to know more. "Why did she die, John? Was she sick a long time?"

"You could say that."

He was sitting cross-legged again. His proud profile cut a clean line against the pale blue sky. As always, his thoughts were masked by his strong, calm exterior.

"Was it the alcoholism?" she asked softly.

He shut his eyes. "Yeah. In the end, her liver failed."

Somehow she knew it would be wrong to say she was sorry. She sat next to him and reached for his hand, cupping her slim fingers around his long, strong ones. Looking down, she noticed the four tiny dots on the back of his hand that she'd once assumed to be birthmarks. Smoothing her thumb over the scar tissue, she wondered how difficult it must have been for him and his father to leave the Dumas ranch every night. What had they gone home to?

"What a waste," she said. "For all of you."

"As far as my mother was concerned, her life was over long before she died. She hadn't appreciated what the consequences of marrying my father would be. If she had, she would've gone somewhere to have her baby, then put it up for adoption. That's what she used to tell me."

Kerry didn't know who to feel more awful for. John the unwanted child, or his father, who would have felt responsible for his wife's unhappiness. "But your parents stayed together?"

"Mom tried to leave a couple of times. Her family and old friends would have nothing to do with her, so she attempted to start out fresh in Reno. But she couldn't cut it. I guess she was too sick. My dad always let her move back in. He never told me why, but I guess it was obligation, plain and simple."

"It wasn't his fault she had a problem with alcohol."

"No, but he blamed himself for marrying her in the first place. Mother was quite young and naïve. She thought her parents would forgive her once the marriage was official. But Dad had lived with prejudice all his life. He knew what a powerful force it could be. I guess he hoped the two of them could rise above it somehow.''

But obviously they hadn't.

"How awful for you.''

"My mother's drinking was something I learned to accept. Frankly, I don't remember her as anything other than a drunk. So when my father let her move back in, I was hardly disillusioned.''

Kerry wasn't sure about that. It seemed to her that John's wounds had settled deep in his bones. Still, in his father's shoes, she could see John making the same choice. To stand by the woman he'd married, for better or worse. Honorable men apparently ran in the Eagle bloodline.

"How did your mother spend her days?'' The kids at school had talked about magic spells and witches' potions. All rubbish, of course. But she had to have done something all those hours alone in the Eagles' isolated cabin.

"She watched TV and drank,'' John said. "My father tried to get her interested in something… anything. He used to buy her books, needlework kits. He was hoping to find some enjoyable way for her to pass the time. She sure never wasted any of it on housekeeping or cooking.''

So, after putting in a long day at the ranch, John and his father had gone home to a dirty, unwelcoming house where they'd had to rustle up their evening meal and prepare for the next day of work.

What a relentless, unhappy grind it must have been. "If she had received treatment…"

"She wouldn't cooperate. You can't beat a dependency like alcoholism if the patient doesn't want to get better. As far as my mother was concerned, she'd ruined her life by marrying my father. There was no hope left."

"What a tragedy."

"Yes, but that's life, right? You didn't have it any easier, with your parents dying when you were only five."

Her parents' death had been a tragedy, no doubt. But for her, the unhappiness had come in one painful event—and her aunt and uncle had been there to help her through it. Of course, Eleanor and Hamilton had been there for John, too. As much as they could be.

"In a way, the Dumases saved us both, didn't they?" No wonder she and John had gravitated toward each other. Two wounded little souls, thrown together by fate.

She stared into the fire, almost hypnotized by the dancing spears of golden flames. "I wish I'd known all this years ago."

"What difference would it have made? Kerry, you were always the best friend I could've asked for. Loyal and honest and tenderhearted. I would have hated for you to feel sorry for me."

And, if she knew anything about John Eagle, it was still the last thing he wanted.

"This meat is going to be inedible if I don't get it off the fire soon."

He removed the spit and spread their roasted dinner on a clean, flat rock. No glaze this time, but John had sprinkled fresh sage as he cooked, and the resulting aroma was tantalizing.

Kerry went to her pack—it, too, had been beat up by her fall, but she found some dried fruit bars to round out their meal.

"Dessert," she said, holding the treat up for him to see.

"I think we've earned it today."

AFTER they'd finished eating, they hit the trail again, making steady progress before the setting sun drove them to camp for the night.

Dark descended quickly in the desert, and with it came cold. John concentrated on making a fire while Kerry rummaged in her pack for a late-night snack.

"I've got some trail mix. Can you make some more of that delicious tea to go with it?"

He couldn't tell if she was joking. "I don't have anything to boil water in." His makeshift utensils had been left in the cave.

"Here's a small pot and an aluminum cup we could share."

"Perfect." He took the implements, then dug in his pockets for some of the herbs he'd gathered while they were walking. He was glad for the tasks—action allowed him to hide his annoyance at himself. Why had he let Kerry goad him into talking about his mother?

Sharing confidences like that wouldn't help him keep his distance—which was what he'd promised himself he would do. Especially when they were secrets he'd never told another soul, not even his grandfather, although he was certain the older man had been aware of everything. One afternoon when he'd been listening to the old shaman's tales, his grandfather had reached over and touched the scars on his hand. There'd been tears in his eyes, but he hadn't spoken.

So often words were unnecessary. John knew that wasn't the popular notion. People thought you needed to discuss everything to death these days, but it wasn't his way. And it wasn't his father's, either. The bond between them had never needed words to cement it.

Which made spewing out his guts to Kerry even more inexplicable. He hated to think he'd been courting her sympathy. Especially now, on this trip, when he was supposed to be putting their relationship into its proper perspective.

He set a flat stone in the fire and placed the full pot of water on it.

Kerry held out the bag of trail mix. "Want some?"

She shifted closer, and he took a handful of the nuts and dried fruit. Her hair was in the same ponytail she'd fashioned that morning. Wispy strands floated around her neck and her ears.

Kerry had pretty little ears, with delicate lobes that

attached straight to the side of her head. Her earrings were studs with a tiny diamond and pearl nestled next to each other. They suited her perfectly.

"Were those a gift from Sutcliff?" He touched the stones gently, then let his finger brush softly over her downy skin.

She fingered the gold studs for a moment, her hand lingering where his had been a mere second before. "No. I bought them myself. For my thirtieth birthday." She smiled. "You know, to cushion the shock."

He was glad they weren't from her boyfriend. He didn't like the idea that the other man might know her well enough to buy something that suited her so exactly.

But that was ridiculous. Evan had to know Kerry better than anyone if they were about to get married.

"Tea's served." He handed her the mug and was ready to caution her about the heat but caught himself in time.

"Thanks." She brought the steaming cup to her lips and peered over the rim at him. Her stunning blue eyes captured his heart, as they always did. He'd never met anyone with eyes like Kerry's. They were more than beautiful. They reflected the essence of her soul—her kindness, her honesty, her ability to see good in the most dire of situations.

John had always been able to read Kerry with one glimpse into those eyes. He watched as she blew away the steam from the tea, all the while keeping her gaze trained on him.

For once, he had no idea what was going on in her head. Only that her thoughts couldn't possibly match his.

Never had he felt his desire for her so keenly. Every cell in his body wanted her. Her thin cotton top gaped at the neck. He could see the smooth tanned skin of her chest, the swell of her breasts, the cotton of her bra.

Her name was singing in his ears. Her breath warmed his face more than the fire. The texture of her skin remained imprinted on his hands.

They'd never even kissed. All these years, and it had never happened, not even once. He'd been careful, oh, so careful, never to cross that boundary with her. He couldn't sabotage all those years of effort with one foolhardy move. But if she leaned even one inch nearer to him, God, he'd be tempted.

"This tea is still too hot." She held out the mug she'd promised to share. "Do you want to try?"

"No, thanks." He looked away, to the fire.

"Are you sure?"

He glanced at her. She wasn't holding the mug. Slowly she placed her hands on his bended knees. Then she did what he'd prayed she wouldn't.

Leaned closer.

CHAPTER SEVEN

BAFFLED—and thrilled—by what she saw in John's usually hard-to-read eyes, Kerry waited. He wanted to kiss her, she was certain, but after several long seconds it became obvious he had no intention of making the first move. Even as his gaze caressed her, devoured her, his hands remained still on the tops of his thighs. He didn't shift toward her by so much as an inch.

The choice was hers. She could pick up their communal mug of tea and start chatting about geology, and he'd catch the beat of the conversation without giving the slightest sign of disappointment or confusion.

On the other hand, she could lean about twelve inches closer and touch her lips to his…and who knew what would happen?

It wasn't right for a woman contemplating marriage to one man to long to kiss another. She knew that. But she hadn't made that final commitment yet, at least not officially.

And if she had lingering questions about her feelings for John, wasn't it best to resolve them now? Before irrevocable actions had been taken?

She'd spoken no vow, given no promise, wore no ring... And John's eyes were calling, daring her to take this ultimate risk with their relationship.

Do it! Closing her eyes, she laid her lips on his. For a second they both froze, and Kerry began to panic. She'd misread the situation. He wasn't at all interested. She needed to pull back and make a joke. But what would she say?

Then John gathered her into his arms and took charge of the situation. In a flash, passion ignited. Genuine, intense, unstoppable passion.

Oh, my... John's kisses told her things she'd never guessed in the many years she'd known him. They told her he *did* think she was beautiful. That he desired her. That these feelings had simmered in him for longer than the day or two they'd been building in her.

When did you first guess? she wanted to ask him. When did he know that the two of them might be more than friends? She'd been blind not to have seen the possibilities before.

John's mouth moved possessively over her face, covering her cheeks, her eyes, her ears, her neck. Every spot he pressed with his lips felt beautiful afterward.

Maybe he'd laced her tea with a sweet poison that thickened her blood, sensitized her nerve endings and rendered her incapable of making any decision other than for their lovemaking to continue.

If so, she wanted a lifetime supply of the intoxicating drug.

He carried her to the sleeping bag, and she barely noticed the transition. Her bruises gave the slightest of protests as he settled her gently, then lay beside her. Cupping her face, he paused.

Asking for permission, she realized. "Yes, John. Oh, yes!"

He kissed her again, and she could barely absorb the pleasure as his hands stroked softly down the length of her arm, only to curl around her neck, then stroke her hair.

A coyote howled. The eerie, high-pitched sound startled them both. She propped herself up on her elbows. John turned, instantly alert. Protectively, he placed an arm over her shoulders as he scanned the world beyond their barely flickering campfire.

"Over there. Next to that boulder." He pointed.

It took almost a minute of concentrated effort before Kerry was able to make out the creature standing not thirty feet away from them. The size of a small, lean dog, the coyote sat perched on his haunches. His eyes glowed orange in the darkness, reflecting the flickering campfire as he watched them.

She shivered, then sat upright, her gaze transfixed. Why was the creature so close? Wasn't it frightened by the flames?

"John, this feels strange."

"Don't worry. He won't come any nearer."

Their physical safety wasn't what concerned her.

How could it? With John's arm around her, it was difficult to imagine something that could truly frighten her.

No, it was the animal's bizarre behavior and something about his face—his expression, if that was possible—that made her uneasy. "Do you see how intently he's looking at us? It's almost like someone sent him with a message and he wants to make sure we get it."

John surprised her by taking her fanciful statement seriously. "Maybe he's a trickster."

"A what?"

"In native American folklore, the trickster can take many forms. A common one is the coyote."

"I've heard the term. What does it mean, exactly?"

"The way I understand it, a trickster is an animal with supernatural capabilities, sent to provide a warning or guidance. Sort of like a guardian angel in your culture, only sometimes with a wicked sense of humor."

"Are these creatures dangerous?"

John shrugged. "Not usually. But the trickster takes on many roles. Commonly he appears as a guide to travelers. Maybe this one is telling us we're on the right path to find out about your parents."

"Do you think?" It was an encouraging idea. From the coyote's calm composure, he didn't seem to be warning them about impending doom.

But she'd spoken too soon. A distant noise she'd

hardly registered crescendoed. The coyote's ears perked, then he darted off. John frowned.

''What the hell?''

The humming, which had first hovered in the air like a swarm of insects, now took on the distinctly mechanical sound of a helicopter. As the intensity of the noise grew, it became clear that at any second the machine would burst into view from behind the sheltering rock walls.

What a bizarre interruption to one of the most erotic moments of her life. John might not see himself as a husband or father, but he was a marvelous lover. Well, she supposed he was, if his kisses were anything to go on.

But their romantic mood was shattered. John had become tense and watchful. The poor coyote had been scared away. Who in the world would be flitting around in a helicopter over Nevada's high desert at this hour of the night?

A crazy but not impossible idea hit her. That couldn't be Evan up there. Could it?

He hadn't been pleased about this expedition of hers. But chartering a helicopter and coming out to look for her...surely that was over the top.

On the other hand, he had a friend in the business, so maybe it was possible. And if it was— She didn't want him to find her. She felt guilty about that, and about how much she'd enjoyed John's kisses.

Still, this was her time, and she wasn't giving up a minute.

Just as bright lights glared from above, she took the pot of hot tea from the flat rock and upended it over the smoldering fire. Whoosh! A cloud of steam rose, then quickly dissipated.

She glanced at John. In the near dark, it was hard to tell for sure, but she thought he gave a small nod of approval.

No one could possibly see them now.

"IF SOMEONE *is* worried about you," John said, not able to voice the name of the most possible candidate—Kerry's almost-fiancé, "it would be nice if we could let them know you're okay."

Kerry hesitated, then went to her pack. She scuffled in it for several minutes before surfacing with the badly battered two-way radio.

"Do you think it'll still work?"

John took the device, and it practically fell apart in his hands. Obviously the radio had been damaged beyond repair in her fall. "Maybe we should've signaled that copter so they'd at least know you were alive."

Kerry shook her head. "They might have taken it as a signal of distress and tried to land. John, I really don't think that could have been Evan. And even if it was, this trip is important to me, and Evan knows it. I won't be stopped."

Considering her nasty fall earlier in the day, John had to admire her fortitude. But getting airlifted out of this place might be the best thing for her. John didn't dare make the suggestion even as he thought about the real reason Kerry was in danger.

He'd kissed her tonight and come damn close to doing much more. The experience had been fantastic.

And changed nothing.

Kerry Dumas belonged to another world, economically, socially, culturally. He knew the trust fund from her parents had paid for her expensive education right on through graduate school, with enough left over that she would never have to worry about money.

He, on the other hand, had needed to work nights and weekends to get through the local community college. Long hours and perseverance had led to making deputy sheriff. But even under a best-case scenario, it was still going to take him years of saving before he could afford to buy some land, let alone build the house he'd always dreamed of.

Kerry didn't need a man who lived under those limitations. Especially considering their backgrounds. And he only had to look at the example his mother had set to be reminded of the dangers of a mixed marriage.

Of course, he was getting ahead of himself. A half hour of necking did not change the course of the stars. Kerry wasn't a deceptive woman, but she was human. That moment between them had arisen out of opportunity and weakness. Once they were back in civilization and her head had cleared, she'd realize Evan was the right man for her. And John would have to let her go, just as he'd done when she'd left the Dumas ranch for those fancy eastern schools.

Still, he had to wonder at the speed with which she'd doused that fire. Why didn't she want Evan to find her? His mind nudged at the problem, presenting several possibilities.

Maybe it was just like she'd said—she was afraid Evan would insist she come home and give up on her quest. But did Evan have that kind of power over her? And if he did, why had she set out on her own in the first place?

John set the broken radio on a flat rock, still considering what had just happened. What if—extremely wild thought here—Kerry had put out that fire because she wanted more time alone with him? An opportunity to explore what had sparked while they were kissing. He knew she'd been as affected as he had been. Could it be she was curious to see what else might develop?

Not for a second did he entertain the possibility that her interest could be any more serious than that. Kerry wasn't a fool. She had to have all the angles figured out, just like he did.

She slid into her sleeping bag for the night, squirming in the confines of the narrow bag and eventually producing her pants, which she rolled up to use as a pillow.

She'd become quiet. Not like her, at all. Was she

worried about the helicopter? Or regretting what had happened between them?

"It doesn't seem fair, me sleeping in relative comfort while you rough it on the rocks."

"I'll be fine," he assured her. "I wanted it this way. Remember?" He'd intended to prove he could survive the way his ancestors had survived. Only it wasn't the physical comforts of modern living he needed to learn to do without.

He wandered several yards from their camp to stow the leftover food in Kerry's backpack, which was hanging on a needle-covered branch of piñon, out of reach from wandering nocturnal creatures.

The stars were out tonight. So many that the display felt almost decadent, like the main strip in Las Vegas at two in the morning. John sighed, then glanced to where Kerry lay. Slow, heavy breathing suggested she'd fallen into an easy sleep. If only oblivion could be that simple for him. He strolled the perimeter of their camp on the lookout for…what? There weren't many predators to worry about in the desert. Unless that coyote came back, and even he was unlikely to pose any threat.

Maybe the uneasiness he felt had nothing to do with the desert. He glanced at the sky, remembering those moments when the helicopter had loomed. That helicopter represented the real world, Kerry's waiting life, and it was a vivid reminder that their time alone in this desert was finite. Only a week or two, at best.

Maybe the helicopter, and whoever was aboard it, hadn't found them yet. But they would, eventually.

IT SEEMED John would never go to sleep. Kerry listened to the quiet step of his feet on the rocky ground, fighting the temptation to call out his name.

She thought she knew why he was so restless. The same reason she was.

Something awesome had happened between them tonight. The imprint of his lips on her skin was still vivid in her mind, but she knew an even more lasting impression had been branded on her heart.

She hadn't wanted their lovemaking to end when it had. In fact, she would open her sleeping bag to him right now, if he'd only ask.

But he didn't. At last she heard him settle on the other side of the fire from her.

She wondered what he was thinking. Did he regret what had happened, or did he, too, wish there'd been no interruption?

Rolling onto her back, Kerry stared into the sky. The brilliance of the stars made her appreciate their isolation from the civilized world of city lights and smog. Out here it was possible to believe that she and John were the only people in the world. Maybe that was why they were experiencing this exciting new attraction.

For the first time since she'd laid her lips against John's, she let herself think about Evan. Closing her eyes, she waited to feel the inevitable guilt. She knew what they'd done—what she'd instigated—was wrong. Not only unfair to Evan, but also very dangerous to the future of her fragile friendship with John.

And yet, she just couldn't seem to regret a second of it.

DREAMS punctuated every moment of Kerry's restless efforts to sleep. At first, they came from her deepest memories of the past.

She was three years old, maybe four, riding a tire swing in the backyard. Her mother stood in front of her, her father behind. They pushed her for what seemed like hours, quietly talking to each other as she grinned with pleasure.

Next she was playing on the kitchen floor while her parents cleaned up from dinner, her mother washing the dishes, her father drying. When the last pot was scrubbed, her mother leaned her back against the sink and worked a dab of lotion into her hands, then rubbed the extra onto Kerry's cheeks. When she was finished, she put on her rings again. First the gold band, then the one with the diamond.

Kerry always woke up at this point in her dream, feeling the same bittersweet sadness. An ache of longing for the parents she had never really known.

Blinking, she gazed into the night with no idea of the time. Out of habit, she twirled the diamond ring she wore on her right hand. Her aunt and uncle had given her this ring on her eighteenth birthday, along with the map. She'd also received her parents' watches, which had long ago ceased operating.

More than any other of her belongings, Kerry treasured her mother's ring and wore it every day. She'd often wondered, though, about the matching wedding band. All her aunt and uncle could tell her was that neither of her parents had been wearing one when their bodies were found.

They'd died in each other's arms. That was something else her aunt and uncle had related, and it was a fact that gave Kerry no small amount of comfort.

All her memories were of her parents together. They'd done everything as a team, from parenting to household chores. Not to mention working in the same office five days a week.

So it was appropriate that in the end, they'd gone as one.

She knew she would have been in their final thoughts and prayers. And she knew, too, that this trip was something they would have wanted her to make. She'd always felt that, partly because she knew her mother had wanted to take her along the first time. Now, lying here in the desert night, her dream still fresh in her mind, she felt the enduring ties that linked the dead to the living.

Although they were gone, they'd never really left her. When she'd been a child, she'd prayed for them every night. Even now, as an adult, she thought of them often.

But she'd never felt closer to either of them than she did right now. She closed her eyes and drifted off to sleep again, almost certain she could smell her father's favorite spearmint candies in the air.

Pink dawn was seeping from the eastern border the next time Kerry awoke from yet another dream—this one not nearly as pleasant. She jerked upright, fighting off the disturbing images.

Her sudden movement woke John. He opened his eyes, instantly alert. "You okay?"

JOHN HAD BEEN aware of Kerry's restless night. He hoped she wasn't regretting their brief taste of lovemaking. Of course, she'd instigated the episode, but he'd taken over pretty quickly. She'd seemed willing at the time, but John knew full well how different these things could seem after the rush of passion was spent.

Not that his passion had been spent. When it came to Kerry, he couldn't imagine it ever would be.

"I had a strange dream." Still encased in her sleeping bag, Kerry sat up, pulling her hair from her face.

"Tell me about it."

"I was in the backyard of my old house, the one I was born in, and my parents were there. They were speaking to me, both at the same time, so I could hardly understand them. Still, I knew they were telling me not to follow the map, to give up and turn back."

She looked not at John's face, but at the fire. It was dead, nothing but a heap of ashes within a circle of stones.

"Then suddenly my parents weren't there at all. Just a spooky old man with a dark, ancient face and small, hooded eyes that scared me with their power."

More precisely, the man in her dream had looked exactly like John's grandfather, but Kerry didn't share this observation in case she offended John. Now that she was an adult, she knew John's grandfather had been a kindhearted and wise man, but the one time she'd met him as a child, she'd been frightened. In her dream, she'd seen the man as he'd seemed to her in her childhood—a representation of everything scary and unknown in the world.

"What happened then?"

She shook her head. "Nothing. I remember thinking, *It's cursed.* And then I woke up."

John started building a new fire, layering sticks of wood with pieces of bark and twigs. When he was done, he lit one of her matches. The bark caught instantly, crackling and shriveling. "Cursed? What do you mean by that, Kerry?"

She was glad it was John sitting next to her, because she'd have been embarrassed to elaborate to anybody else. "That marking at the end of the trail— whatever it's meant to represent. I'm being ridiculous, aren't I?"

She wanted him to tell her she was, but John's expression remained serious. "I'm not so sure. If your father's drawing is related to that native legend I told you the other night, it's possible an ancient shaman placed some sort of protective spell or curse on that spot.''

''You're serious?''

''Serious might be stretching it. I'm just saying it's possible. I'm still a skeptic at heart, but who am I to judge? Maybe your parents died because they attempted to disturb an ancient native artifact.''

A shiver of fear raced up Kerry's backbone. ''You don't really believe that.''

John shrugged. ''Five years ago, I would've said no. I spent a lot of time with my grandfather in the last few years of his life, though. And to him, dreams were more meaningful than real life. I'm sure he would think your dream was something we should take seriously.''

''Stop it, John. You're really scaring me now.'' This was worse than ghost stories around a campfire at midnight. John seemed to be giving credence to these wild ideas.

''You forget that I'm a scientist,'' she continued. ''And this isn't *Raiders of the Lost Ark*. In all probability, we're talking about the remnants of some natural disaster. Fascinating from a historical and scientific perspective, but nothing to inspire something as melodramatic as an ancient native curse.''

''If you're so sure the idea of a curse is bunk, then why are you shivering?''

''I'm cold.'' And she was, but that didn't mean John wasn't correct. The truth was, the dream had affected her, and on one level his interpretation of it rang true.

"And I'm *not* giving up."

"I never thought you would."

"But you want me to."

"Kerry, I'm not saying I believe in that old legend or the possibility of a curse. You were the one who had the dream."

"Yes."

She unzipped her sleeping bag and pulled on her pants. Then she hunted down her map.

"How far can we make it today?" Finished with tending his fire, John came to join her. His long brown fingers touched hers as he pointed out their current position.

She was amazed how close to their goal they'd come. "We should get there by tomorrow."

"I think so," he agreed.

Excitement zinged through the cold and exhaustion she felt. Tomorrow all her questions would be answered. And she was glad John would be there to share the moment with her. Carefully she folded the map and returned it to the plastic pouch.

They had tea and beef jerky for breakfast. After cleaning up their camp, they set out at a fair pace.

"Sore?" John asked her, his gaze on the tears in her pants.

"A little."

"Well, no need to push too hard today."

They stopped just past noon and waited out the

hottest hours. Kerry thought she'd be tired after her restless night. But she couldn't stop watching John, wondering what he was thinking.

She wanted him to talk about what had happened between them last night. She wanted an intimate word, a knowing smile.

But he was her old pal John again. A dependable friend. A trustworthy travel companion.

A couple hours before the sun was due to set, he suggested they get moving again. They traveled quickly, wasting no breath on unnecessary chitchat. After about half an hour, Kerry became aware of a restless wind and mounting clouds, both pushing in from the west.

"Another storm?" she wondered.

"I think so. Let's see if we can find some shelter higher up on this mountain."

But before they could find anything, the storm struck. A sizzling bolt of lightning traveled across the sky from one black cloud to the next. Seconds later, the ground was shaking from the crash of thunder, and the rain started.

For a second Kerry froze. Then John grabbed her hand.

"That sounded close." He shouted to be heard above the storm. "We need to find shelter."

CHAPTER EIGHT

TEN MINUTES LATER, the storm reached its full potential. John and Kerry found protection from the worst of the rain and wind in a small hollow in the leeward side of a curved rock formation. Soon John had a small fire sputtering in front of them.

It seemed to Kerry that even between the claps of thunder, she could hear the sizzle of supercharged electricity in the air.

John pulled several sticks of dry wood from the copious pockets of his hiking pants and set them on the smoldering kindling.

"Smart." She'd noticed him stooping to pick up dry sticks occasionally throughout the day. Now she understood why.

"At least the wood is dry." With his pockets emptied, he sat next to her. Backs to the mountain, shoulders touching, they were quiet for several minutes.

Kerry closed her eyes and leaned her head against the rock. It seemed that the time lag between the flashes of lightning and the booming of thunder was gradually increasing. A toasty warmth began to build from their small campfire. But Kerry found more comfort in the heat of John's body next to hers.

"You're shivering," he said. "Why don't you crawl into your sleeping bag for a while?"

"What about you? You're soaked, too."

John didn't say anything.

Wearily, she reached for the backpack she'd tossed to the ground. She pulled the sleeping bag from the waterproof cover, then, concealed by the darkness, she doffed her clothing and dived into the lofty softness.

"You're right. This does feel better."

"Good."

Prudence dictated that she say nothing further. But prudence had never been Kerry's strong point. "You know, there's room for two in here."

John unfolded his legs and got to his feet. Kerry's heart skipped a beat. Was he taking her up on her offer? But no, he'd merely gone to her pack.

"Hungry?"

"Starved," she admitted.

"Guess we'll have to eat your provisions tonight. I'll never find anything to hunt in this weather." He shuffled around in the compartment where she kept the food supplies. "What'll it be? Beef jerky or trail mix?"

She groaned. "What I wouldn't give for a plate of fresh pasta and a crisp, tangy salad. Or better yet, a bowl of thick, steaming soup." Remembering how delicious his catch the other morning had been, she asked, "Do you cook much at home?"

"Not from recipes. When I make a chili or a stew, it's toss in a little of this and a little of that."

"Sounds very creative." And delicious. Her mouth watered just thinking of all those cooked vegetables and spices. "If I could have anything I wanted right now, it would be Aunt Eleanor's summer soup. Do you remember?"

"I do. It was fantastic. Do you know how to make it?"

"You bet. I made her teach me before I moved out. First she sautés onions and garlic, then adds grated zucchini and chopped red pepper. Once the veggies are golden brown and fragrant, she tosses in masses of juicy chopped tomatoes—fresh from the garden, still warm from the sun."

"Oh, man, I remember those tomatoes."

"Then fresh basil, salt, ground pepper…the whole thing simmers for about twenty minutes and is then pureed. For the finishing touch, she blends in dollops of tangy cream cheese and just a dab of honey."

"God, I can almost taste it."

She could, too. And it was killing her. "Tell me your favorite recipe."

"Well, like I said, I don't follow the same rules every time, but when I make my corn bread, I add grated cheese, fresh corn kernels and chopped chili peppers. And I use the richest sour cream money can buy."

"Oh, John." She inhaled deeply, almost imagining

she could smell something baking in the air. "This is driving me crazy."

"Me, too."

Kerry swallowed as she stared into John's dark eyes. He'd crouched in front of her to pass her the beef jerky, and they were very, very close.

"I love it when you talk food to me, Kerry," he said softly.

Tentatively she held out her hand. He pressed the stick of beef jerky into her palm.

"Your recipe or mine?" she asked.

"TELL ME your favorite dessert."

John wanted to say *you*. He wanted to be the big, bad wolf and gobble Kerry up like she was Red Riding Hood's basket of goodies.

How had he got to this point? After last night he'd sworn he wouldn't let himself be ruled by temptation. The only reason these sparks were flying between them was that they were isolated from the real world. The more indulgence he allowed himself, the harder it would be returning to that real world in the end.

But hell. How could he care about the real world when he had the black night of the desert above him and the girl of his dreams at his side?

The rain had stopped. He could hear the echoing of thunder, but the sound was traveling from far down in the valley.

Food, he reminded himself. They were talking about food. His favorite dessert.

"Again, I'd go back to your aunt Eleanor's kitchen. Remember those pastries she used to bake? Buttery and flaky with that rich vanilla cream filling? You'd bite into them and the cream would spill out onto your chin."

"Oh, yeah, and they were covered in chocolate sauce. She used to let me help. I'd dip in my spoon, then drizzle the thick fudge sauce over each pastry. I think she used bitter chocolate to contrast with the sweetness of the cream."

John clenched his hands over his knees. Kerry looked as if she was being brought to orgasm as she swooned over her aunt's old recipe. Knowing she was next to naked in that sleeping bag made the comparison even more appropriate. God, this was the sweetest torture he'd ever put himself through.

"Her bumbleberry pie, too. Remember, John? You'd cut into it with a fork and all those tart, red and blue berries would come spilling out."

"Please, Kerry. I can't take much more of this."

"I know exactly how you feel."

John sincerely doubted that.

"Of course, there are substitutions for good food," she added, proving him wrong. With her head resting on her bent knees—a small hill in her sleeping bag—she gazed at him. A longing as feminine as her curled, dark eyelashes emanated from her. Her lids fluttered slightly as she focused on his mouth. Was she remembering their kisses last night? Her expression was dreamy. Inviting.

John decided it was up to him to insert some reality into the situation. "We didn't see that helicopter today."

Kerry dropped her gaze to the rock floor. "No."

"Do you think he's given up?"

"It may not have been Evan."

"But if it was, do you think he'll be back? More to the point, do you *hope* he'll come back?"

KERRY CONSIDERED John's question carefully. She hadn't thought of Evan much today. She pictured him in her mind, his familiar features, his medium-size, sturdy build. She saw him at his desk at the office, head bent over paperwork, frowning in concentration.

In the space of only a few days, she'd experienced nothing less than a revolution of feelings. Suddenly she could no longer remember why she'd wanted to marry the man.

Yes, they had common interests, but nothing compared with what she and John had.

Yes, she'd been attracted to him once, but again, with nothing of the passion she felt for the man beside her right now.

For some reason, she could see that John fought his feelings for her. She wished she could understand why, but really, the reason didn't matter.

She couldn't promise to marry one man when she'd never felt more alive than when kissing another.

As she contemplated John's question, her mind was clear, her answer unequivocal.

''No, I'm not hoping Evan will be back. I've decided not to marry him.''

As soon as the words were out, she waited for panic to strike. She was making a mistake she might regret later. Already she was thirty. What if she never found the right man? These questions had plagued her for weeks.

But she felt no anxiety. Only calm certainty. She didn't want to marry Evan.

Really, there was no other conclusion that made sense. The situation between her and John was spiraling out of control.

And she wanted it to.

Knowing all this, how could she possibly entertain the idea of marriage to Evan Sutcliff?

''You're sure?'' John had taken off his wet shirt but still wore his trousers. She loved the look of his powerful brown chest, the sculpted muscles at his shoulders and biceps.

''Two days ago I wasn't. Now I am. I think part of the reason I wanted to go on this trip by myself was my own uncertainty. If I'd felt one hundred percent sure of Evan, why wouldn't I have told him about the map and invited him along?'' It was weird to second-guess her actions. But for some reason, she hadn't allowed herself to see the truth before.

''What about turning thirty and wanting to start a family?''

''I still want that.'' Oh, God, she was too bold. That had come out almost as brazen as a proposal.

And John hadn't said a word about what had happened between them last night. She couldn't believe their kisses had been trivial to him. But she'd still like to hear exactly how he felt.

"Do you regret kissing me, John?"

As always, he wouldn't be forced. "I suppose that you do."

"Of course not. I wish we'd tried it sooner. Years sooner." Why hadn't they? She didn't have to think too hard to find the answer. She'd pegged John in the role of childhood friend. But here, in the desert, she'd seen him as a man for the first time. A powerful, virile, desirable man.

"Kerry, be careful what you say." In the dim light from the fire, she saw him give her a frank, masculine appraisal. She loved seeing how desire narrowed his eyes and softened his lips.

"I don't want to be careful."

Since she'd undressed, she'd been cinching up her sleeping bag modestly with one hand. Now she deliberately let go, and the quilted fabric fell into her lap.

"Kerry…" He cupped his hands gently on her bare shoulders.

Heat swirled between her legs, and anticipation fizzed through her veins. The night air was cooling, but she burned hot as he eased the cotton straps of her bra off her shoulders. Her skin sizzled wherever he touched. His hands slid down her shoulders and her back to unfasten the clasp of her bra.

He didn't rush. She'd been desperate to kiss him,

but, mesmerized by his touch, she couldn't find the willpower to move her mouth next to his. Instead, she held her breath for the moment he would touch her bare breasts.

When it finally happened, the pleasure made her dizzy. She whispered for him not to stop as his thumbs brushed over her nipples again and again.

Then he kissed her and, like before, she fell into a trance. Nothing mattered except John and her and this wonderful hot magic they created together.

It was crazy that so many years had passed and she'd never guessed it could be like this with John. Every sensation he brought her felt beautiful, true and right. Before he'd even touched her, she'd known that this time they would love each other completely. She'd seen the promise in his eyes and could only hope that her gaze gave him the same message.

She unzipped her sleeping bag, making room for him. Peeking out from the last straggling storm clouds, a handful of stars illuminated the bronze perfection of his body as he stepped out of his trousers.

Every inch of the man was perfect. And he made her feel perfect, as well, as he caressed every inch of her, right down to her poor misshapen foot. No spot seemed too insignificant for him to notice.

"John?"

"Hmm?"

"I'm glad it's happening this way between us. Here, in the desert. Just stars and clean air and you and me."

He'd kissed her arm all the way from her shoulder to the very tip of her baby finger. Now he brushed his lips over first one nipple, then the other.

"I'm glad, too. Kerry, are you ready?"

She nodded. She'd been ready for ages, yet hadn't felt any need to rush, either.

John was a magnificent lover. Only at one point, at the very end, did she feel anything other than pure delight. As her climax began a long crescendo, she felt a split second of panic.

This is too good. It can't last.

Then the pleasure took over, and John shuddered in her arms. She called out his name, but the sound was lost as a soulful howl punctured the evening quiet.

The coyote is back.

She gasped and tensed. John pulled her to his chest tenderly.

"Sounds like our trickster," he said.

"You really think it's the same animal?"

Of course, he couldn't know, but she discovered that she liked the idea. She wanted to believe that somewhere in these vast, wild mountains, someone, or something, was looking out for them.

The coyote yipped again, and Kerry cuddled next to John as he wrapped the sleeping bag over her naked body. The animal sounded close, very close, but she wasn't afraid.

She felt protected in John's arms, safe and loved. Even though he hadn't said a single word about his feelings, she knew he wouldn't have made love to her if he didn't care deeply.

"I love you, John." He was such a special person. She couldn't imagine what her life would have been like without him in it.

It didn't worry her when he failed to answer with endearing words of his own. She knew that what counted with John were actions, not talk. And he'd already shown her exactly how he felt.

Satisfied with that, she fell asleep.

MORNING seemed to come with Kerry's very next breath. But she'd slept for hours. The sun was already warming the thin desert air.

Alone in her sleeping bag, Kerry felt peaceful and happy. John must be out hunting for breakfast. That was good. She didn't want to face another meal of beef jerky or dried fruit.

Propping herself onto her elbows, she examined their makeshift camp more carefully. Last night's fire had been rekindled, and her pack hung from the branch of a nearby pine.

Kerry dressed quickly, rolled up her sleeping bag, then walked some distance from the camp before finding a private place to relieve herself. Seeing no obvious source of water—although John had filled their canteens either late last night or earlier this morning—she used the water in her drinking bag for washing up.

Today they would reach the end of the trail. That

knowledge should have preoccupied her, but what had happened between her and John last night suddenly seemed much more important.

She was over her head, and it wasn't the first time she'd felt this way with John....

CHAPTER NINE

IN THE BACK of Johnny's father's pickup, the winding gravel roads felt a lot rougher than they did from the cushioned passenger seat of a car. Under the orange tarp where Kerry hid, the air stank as bad as in the dirt cellar where Aunt Eleanor stored the fall potatoes and the jars of strawberry jam and pickles she canned every summer.

Kerry lifted the corner of the tarp. The canvas flapped madly in her hand as the sweet evening air swished by her. Although it was hard to breathe and her knees hurt, pressed against the hard cold metal of the truck bed, she was happy, excited.

Just wait until Johnny found out what she'd done. He'd think she was so smart. Soon they would be at the Eagles' cabin. She'd stay hidden in here until Johnny came out of his house after dinner.

Kerry clutched the bag of provisions she'd gathered. Everything Johnny had said they'd need, she had. Even the knife.

The truck slowed. Afraid Mr. Eagle had noticed the fluttering tarp, Kerry flattened herself against the truck bed, pulling the stinky orange canvas over her. But the truck didn't stop; they were just turning a corner. As the vehicle rattled over some cattle guards, Kerry felt like a corn kernel being popped on the stove.

A few more minutes passed, then abruptly the truck slowed again. She risked lifting the tarp off her face for a peek. The air smelled different here, and there were fewer trees. They were in the mountains, she realized.

The grinding of a changing gear was followed immediately by a small jerk as the truck prepared to stop. Finally! She wanted to peer out but decided she'd better wait until she was certain both Mr. Eagle and Johnny were in the house.

She listened to the doors of the cab open and close, followed by another, unexpected sound. Barking. So Johnny had a dog.

She hoped he was friendly.

"Hey, Friday! Good boy, Friday!" That was Johnny, talking to his dog. Kerry listened to footsteps moving away from her. Another door opened and closed—this one to the house. After a full minute of silence, she risked taking a look.

Gosh. The Eagles' house was awfully little. Tiny, really, compared with the ranch house where Kerry lived with her aunt and uncle. And not exactly good to look at. Rough, unpainted wood, no flowers, dirty windows.

Kerry wished she could see in those windows. She was curious about what was going on inside. Was Johnny's mother home? Were they having supper?

Why was everyone so quiet? Someone was always going in or out, shouting or singing or just banging around at the ranch.

If it hadn't been for that dog, she'd have hopped out of the back of the truck to get a better look. But while the dog had gone inside with John and his dad, Kerry knew he'd start barking if he heard her moving around outside. Then Johnny would blame her for being foolish and impatient and wrecking everything.

Eventually Kerry grew bored of watching the quiet house where nothing seemed to happen. She threw the tarp off her body and settled on the hard metal floor of the truck bed. Staring at the wispy clouds, she searched for signs of her parents. They were up there, she knew, in heaven. Maybe they'd turned into clouds. Scrutinizing the scattered formations, she spotted one that looked like a mommy in a long flowing dress....

She guessed she fell asleep, because the next time she blinked, it was dark and she couldn't see the clouds anymore. Lights shone in Johnny's house around the edges of the curtains. They didn't seem to fit the shapes of the windows very well.

Kerry rolled over impatiently. What was taking Johnny so long? She tried imagining what the Eagles were eating for supper. There weren't any smells in the air. Maybe they were having leftovers from yesterday.

Pulling at the zipper on her pack she unearthed a bag of cookies she'd snitched from Aunt Eleanor's kitchen. For a while she munched quite happily, then she got bored again. She really wanted a glass of milk. And a bathroom.

Suddenly an awful howling came from the house, like a wild animal crying. Kerry crawled under the tarp. After a few minutes, the sound stopped, and the house returned to its former stillness.

But the air felt different, and Kerry could still hear the spooky wailing inside her head. She longed to get moving, to run away from this place.

But Johnny had the map. She had to wait.

Finally, she saw him slip out the back door. He was wearing the same clothes as earlier but had wrapped some stuff into a blanket, which he'd slung over his shoulder.

After grabbing her pack, she slid on her bottom to the back of the truck. Up and over the tailgate, then she jumped off the back bumper to the ground. She lost her balance and scraped her palms on the dirt road. A few rocks bit into her skin, but nothing bled. She dusted off her jeans, then began to run.

Johnny turned, his expression gratifyingly astonished.

"What're you doing here?"

"I was hiding in the back of your dad's truck." She'd expected him to give her a grin, a pat on the back. She'd thought he'd be glad.

But he seemed a little mad. "Aw, Kerry. Now you've ruined everything."

"What do you mean?" Johnny was her friend.

Why wasn't he glad to see her? She wondered if it had something to do with the way he'd been squirreling away food earlier that day. Something was going on that he hadn't told her about.

"Oh, heck. Forget it. Just go back to the house and knock on the door." He shook his head. "No. That won't work, either." He pushed his dark hair off his forehead, glanced at the mountains, then at her.

"I guess you'd better come with me," he said. "But make sure you keep up. And don't get lost."

JOHN HAD OFTEN baffled her, Kerry realized. She waited for him to make the first move when he returned to camp with their breakfast, but he barely seemed to notice her. His catch of the day had been cleaned and skinned and was ready for the spit. Efficiently he propped the meat over the fire, then started brewing tea.

"Well, today is the big day," he said. "Excited?"

Somehow she'd expected more from him. If not an endearment or an embrace, then a special smile or at least a warm glint in his eye. John was acting as if nothing out of the ordinary had happened last night.

But maybe at this point their quest demanded all his attention.

"I'm not as excited as I expected," she admitted.

"Why not?"

"I'm not sure I want this trip to be over."

"It won't be. Even if we find Black Valley today,

we still have to make our way back to your car. We'll be roughing it for at least another three days.''

''And *nights,*'' she added suggestively.

John didn't say a word. Didn't even glance at her.

Something was wrong. She remembered her moment of panic last night. The magic between them had been so powerful she'd been afraid it wouldn't last.

But now it was daylight, and she was awake. And still she felt the magic.

Didn't John?

From the way he was behaving, nothing could be more important than the meat sizzling on the spit, the water about to boil for tea. His focus on practical matters left her unsure how to act or what to say.

She decided it was safest to be practical, too. So she consulted the map one more time. This last leg of their journey was the most crucial of the entire expedition. And would also be the most difficult.

Her father's trail followed the ridge of mountains they were on for several more miles. At the end of a series of switchback turns, the solid black line became a dash that passed through what appeared to be a mountain wall. Beyond the dash was Black Valley and the sketch that marked the end of the trail.

What, exactly, did that dashed line represent? A path? A secret passageway?

As she pondered the possibilities, John served breakfast. She nibbled directly off the skewer and sipped from the mug they shared. Despite the simple fare, she enjoyed every bite.

"This is good." The sun was still low enough to be merely warm, not scorching. The view from her perch on a waist-high flat rock would have graced a travel brochure cover. "I'm not in any hurry to return to civilization."

"Don't you miss your modern conveniences? Like fresh-brewed coffee and running water?"

She sighed, thinking of the deep, slope-backed tub in her condo, the plentiful supply of hot water and bath salts. "I suppose I do," she admitted. "But there have been compensations."

John's expression turned blank.

Kissing you. Being with you.

She stared mutely at him, willing him to acknowledge what had happened between them last night. When he didn't, she couldn't hold back any longer.

"John, last night was totally amazing. Don't you think?" Watching his profile, she could not mistake the way the muscles in his neck and jaw tightened at her words.

"It was just one night."

His words shocked her. He couldn't mean them.

But then why was he staring at his feet instead of her?

She felt an overwhelming, crushing hurt.

John didn't care, after all. Last night had been just another night. And what had she been? Just another girl, she supposed.

Her hurt turned quickly to anger.

"Why are you being such a jerk? I can't say I expected you to gather a bouquet of wildflowers and sing a love ballad this morning, but I did think you'd at least look me in the eye."

Once started, she couldn't stop. "Did we do something wrong? Something to be ashamed of? I told you I wasn't going to marry Evan. I meant it."

Oh, God, she'd allowed herself to get all fired up. Now all she wanted to do was cry. Forget the damned breakfast! She tossed her portion of John's hard-won roasted meat onto the open flames, then dashed her tea on top of it.

The fire sizzled but didn't go out.

She grabbed her pack and slipped the straps over her shoulders. Feeling the weight settle on her back, she fought an unexpected weariness. Her muscles ached, her bruises were tender, and her bad foot throbbed. And she had a whole day of trekking ahead of her.

With John. Whom she couldn't even stand to look at right now. She stomped toward the path they'd broken off from yesterday, but after only a few steps John's hand fell on her shoulder.

She froze.

"I am a jerk. You're right."

One long arm came around her waist. The other squeezed her shoulder.

"I'm sorry, Kerry. I know it must seem as if I'm being cold and unfeeling. But I have no choice. There are too many factors I have no control over. That you can't control, either.''

''I don't understand.'' Closing her eyes, she leaned into him. He was as solid as a mountain wall behind her. One of the sobs she'd been repressing hiccuped in her chest.

''We're different, Kerry. Too different. You were raised by the man who owned the ranch. I'm just the son of the hired help.''

''What does that matter? People don't think that way anymore.''

''What about all the money your parents left for you? I'm just a working man, Kerry.''

She swiveled, bringing her eyes to his chest. She stepped backward. ''For heaven's sake, John. It's not like I'm a millionaire. I work, too. I'm hardly accustomed to an extravagant lifestyle.'' She could tell by the stubborn set of his mouth that none of her words had reached him. Once again, he refused to answer.

''You're just making up excuses. Some way to pawn me off without admitting that you're not interested in anything long term.''

His eyes reminded her of two perfect samples of polished onyx. They were as beautiful and as cold as gemstones on display in a jeweler's cabinet.

''I don't need excuses, Kerry. Just look at the color of my skin next to yours. Nothing either of us says or does can change that.''

''So what? John, I love the color of your skin. It's beautiful.''

"Don't be naive. This has nothing to do with shades of brown and everything to do with people's attitudes. Don't kid yourself into believing racism is a problem of the past. Believe me, I run into one example of it or another almost every week of my life."

He removed his hands, letting them drop to his sides. "The differences between you and me matter, Kerry. Last night I failed you and I failed myself. It should never have happened."

"YOU DIDN'T fail me last night, John. You're failing me now."

Kerry didn't understand. This was *his* test, and he'd come up way, way short. He'd known from the first moment he'd seen her in his cave that he was meant to resist her. That this was the method the spirits had chosen to challenge his worth as a man.

And he'd lasted only two nights.

"You'll see more clearly once you get home," he said. Surrounded by family and friends, she'd realize where she belonged and where he didn't.

She pressed her mouth closed, lips trembling like a hurt child's. His answer was clearly not what she'd wanted him to say.

"I suppose you're giving me the brush-off. In the nicest possible John way."

"Kerry, I'm not saying I didn't enjoy what happened between us last night." Enjoy? It had been like heaven to hold her and touch her and kiss her. To tell her so would only compound his errors. "But I don't think a casual affair would be a good thing. Not for you, not for our friendship."

And definitely not for him. To have Kerry completely, and then let her go, would kill him.

"When did I give you the impression I was interested in a casual affair?"

"Never," he admitted. "But that's all we could ever have. I'm not good enough for you, Kerry. That's what it boils down to."

"*Good enough?* John, you make me want to scream. You're good enough for anyone you want. And any woman would be lucky to have you."

This was not a conversation he wanted to have with her. But he was backed into a corner. He might as well answer.

"Kerry, I know what I'm talking about. My father married a white woman. The difference in their skin colors destroyed the happiness of our whole family."

Kerry pushed against his chest. "It doesn't have to be that way."

"Maybe not, but it often is."

"With you and me, it would be different."

You and me. Such seductive words. But John knew better than to buy into the dream. "My mother's family cut off all contact after her marriage."

"So?"

"Your family—" He began patiently.

"Stop right there. You're not assuming my family would react the same way? That Eleanor and Hamilton and my cousins are nothing but a bunch of big-ots?''

''The Dumases are fine people. I'm not arguing about that.'' But Kerry was underestimating the pro-tective instincts of the people who had raised her.

''I don't think they'd welcome news of a relation-ship between you and me,'' he continued honestly.

''That's ridiculous!''

He shook his head at her innocence. ''Why do you suppose Zach made a point of telling me you were about to be engaged to Sutcliff?''

Kerry took a few seconds to answer. ''I imagine he was just filling you in because of your close connec-tion to the family.''

''I don't think so, Kerry. Zach wasn't filling me in, he was warning me off.''

''I don't believe it.''

He clamped his mouth shut stubbornly.

''You're just making excuses. Blaming Zach in-stead of taking the responsibility yourself. If you're not interested in me *that* way, then you should have the courage to just say so.''

''Don't be absurd. Do you think I could have made love to you the way I did last night if I wasn't inter-ested?'' He'd never shared so much passion with any woman. Because he'd never felt a fraction of what he felt for Kerry for another woman.

''If that's true, John, then maybe you should kiss me again.''

He turned his face away. "You haven't listened to a word I've said."

"I've listened," she insisted. "Your mother was an alcoholic. I understand how awful that was for your family. But blaming all her problems on her interracial marriage isn't right, either."

Kerry was wrong. Anyone who hadn't experienced a childhood like his could never understand. Even trying to explain was senseless.

CHAPTER TEN

As soon as KERRY mentioned his mother, she could see John's defenses slip into place. He blanked out the expression on his face and relaxed his body posture.

Kerry watched with folded arms. "I guess in your opinion I should marry Evan. Is that what you want?"

"God, no."

He sounded appalled. The hypocrite.

"Evan has all the qualities you seem to think are so important. He has a first-class education, wealthy parents and a promising career at the Land Bureau. And he's *white*."

"Fine then. Marry him." With a fierce kick he dislodged one of the stones circling the old fire.

Kerry joined in with the hard toe of her boot, helping to scatter the rocks and distribute the ashes. When they left, the landscape would not be scarred by the night they'd spent taking shelter here.

But her heart would forever bear the marks.

"I don't see what's so wrong about not being rich," she said, breaking into John's sullen mood. "Or what's so awful with choosing law enforcement, rather than geology, for a career."

"I'm not ashamed of who I am," John said tersely.

She didn't answer. It seemed to her that he was. Or else he was covering up the real reason he didn't want to get involved with her.

At any rate, it was pointless to argue. She'd been trying for almost half an hour and hadn't gotten him to concede a single issue.

"We should get moving," she said. They'd wasted too much time already.

He took the lead, and Kerry didn't argue. Although it was true that she wasn't in any hurry to get back to the everyday conveniences of life in Reno, this trip was taking its toll on her body. A day of rest would have been heaven. But clearly John wanted this excursion to end as soon as possible. She wasn't going to be the one to slow him down.

It would have helped if she'd eaten her breakfast. Too late now to regret tossing it into the fire. She'd snack later, once they'd made some headway.

Unfortunately for her, John set a grueling pace. From the stiff set of his shoulders, he was still angry. Thinking back to her initial naïve hope that this time together would help them recapture their earlier friendship, she felt like crying. After last night, their friendship was toast. They might be able to put on an act for the occasional Dumas gathering. But anything more would be impossible.

Kerry kicked at a loose stone in her path. This journey was turning out to be a real success. So far she'd bruised most of her body parts, lost a fiancé and her best friend, too. At this rate, the treasure at the end of the trail was likely to be a haphazard arrangement of ordinary rocks—nothing of any significance, geological or cultural.

They trekked in single file, and eventually Kerry could no longer ignore the growing dryness of her mouth and throat. She'd been so angry she'd forgotten to ask John where to fill her canteen. Several times, he'd stopped to take long pulls from his water bottle. As he paused at the lip of an uncharted canyon, she expected him to do the same thing.

Instead, he put a finger to his lips and motioned her to join him. She crept up quietly, not sure what to expect. He held out an arm as a barricade, and when she drew close, he grabbed one of the straps on her backpack. Suddenly, Kerry saw why.

The ground sank, just a foot from where they were standing, into a narrow canyon about thirty feet deep. One more step forward and she would have tumbled over the edge. Secured by John's grip on her pack, Kerry leaned over to see where a careless traveler might end up, and spotted a wide ledge about eight feet down. In all probability, the unlucky victim would not get off injury free. Eight feet was quite a drop.

Enough to break a leg?

The vision of her father sprawled helpless on that ledge caused her to falter with dizziness. John's hand pulled her back tightly.

"Look over there."

She risked another glance and noticed what had caught his attention. On the patchy grassland at the canyon bottom roamed a herd of wild horses.

They were a scraggly lot, their colors varying from dirty vanilla to sorrel to almost black. Not large animals, they lacked the perfect bone structure of their thoroughbred cousins, yet their proud spirits and graceful movements made them all the more magnificent.

The sight swept Kerry's dark imaginings away. She felt cleansed, uplifted, as she always did when she spotted one of the elusive herds.

Her love for these creatures was a significant reason she'd chosen to work for the Land Bureau after graduation. She wanted to be part of the system that protected them. During the twenties and thirties, the wild horse and burro population in Nevada had been almost wiped out by mustangers who rounded them up for such base purposes as pet food and fertilizer. Fortunately, those days were long gone, but the wild horses faced other dangers.

"There's a drinking hole down there." John spoke quietly, barely moving his mouth. The stallion's senses were acute. Any sign of trouble and he'd have the herd moving with one shrill command.

At the mention of the drinking hole, Kerry thought of her empty water bottle with resignation. The canyon floor might as well have been the water station at her office.

As they watched, the mares and foals lined up at

the water's edge. Rigid rules governed the social structure of the herd, and this included drinking order, as well. After the mothers and their babies were finished, it would be the colts' and fillies' turn. Last to be satiated would be the stallion.

They stood watching, spellbound, for several long minutes. John's hand eventually slipped off the strap of her pack and onto her shoulder. She felt his firm grip, and her spirits lifted. Maybe, just maybe, they could sort this mess out.

Kerry sensed him looking at her and turned her head. He smiled, and she knew he was equally affected by the sight they were witnessing. Gazing into the canyon, she noted it was finally the stallion's turn. Every few seconds he lifted his grand head from the water and checked carefully for signs of trouble.

With their thirst quenched, a couple of the colts began to run in circles, nosing each other, backing away, then going through the whole routine again. Almost like children playing tag, Kerry thought, amused.

"We should move on," John whispered.

She knew he was right, even though she could have happily watched the herd all morning. As they stepped back from the canyon, her foot dislodged a stone. It tumbled forward, then over the edge.

The stallion drew up tall and swung his head in their direction. For one second he was silent. Kerry held her breath, feeling as if the proud leader was making eye contact with her. Then the animal let out a loud, wild cry. As Kerry shivered in response, the pack pulled together. Straggling foals ran to their mothers, following them as they galloped up the sloping approach on the opposite side of the canyon. Within a minute, the entire herd had disappeared.

"Wasn't that something?" Kerry sighed. The deserted canyon was still and empty. Almost as if the horses had never been there.

John reached to the opening of her backpack. "Mind if I check the map?"

"Go ahead." She waited patiently while he pulled open the separate compartment where she kept the plastic-wrapped package.

"Let's take this to the shade."

A few feet away, a cone-shaped rock formation offered some protection from the sun. Kerry followed John, then kneeled beside him as he spread the paper flat on the rock floor.

"I was wondering what this marking was." John pointed out a scribble that looked like an irregular W to Kerry. Next to it was a red circle.

She pointed out the circle. "Why the different color ink?"

"My guess is that mark wasn't made by your father."

Which had to mean… Oh Lord. "You think this is the spot where they…where the search party found their bodies?"

The spooky sensation she'd experienced at the edge of the canyon returned. Down to the marrow of her bones, she felt her hunch was correct. This was where her parents had died.

She had to share her thoughts with John. "When I first saw that canyon, I wondered what would happen to someone who fell over. Did you see the ledge about eight feet down?"

"I did."

"That could be how my father broke his leg."

"It's possible."

Kerry played the scenario through in her mind. "My mother must have dragged him up from the ledge. They would have headed for the nearest shelter."

Which would most likely have been here, this spot she and John had selected to take refuge from the desert heat. The rock formation offered shade but precious little else. No water, no food, none of the basics of survival.

She closed her eyes and searched inward for a connection to her parents. Her memories of them were so vague. But she had pictures and even some home movies that she watched from time to time. So she could visualize their faces, even imagine she could hear their voices.

She wanted to believe that their last hours had brought them peace. They'd been together, and they would have known Hamilton and Eleanor would take care of her. But something kept jarring her vision. A nagging, ugly, anxious feeling she wanted to ignore.

"John, why do you think my father made the map

with such a lack of detail? I know he wasn't an expert, but so many of his markings are vague. And why didn't he include a key to explain his little symbols and abbreviations?''

John folded the map. "Good question. Perhaps he didn't want to make this an easy place to find.''

"Could he have been worried about someone in particular? Someone who knew about the native American profile? Someone my father didn't trust.''

"Possibly. A co-worker, I suppose, or a friend.''

"According to my uncle, my parents were very secretive about this trip. That's why it took so long to find their...bodies. They hadn't let anyone know where they were going. All they told Hamilton and Eleanor was their starting point and the date they expected to return.''

If the search party had had a clearer idea of where to look for them, the searchers might have arrived in time to save them. This was one of many variables that sometimes kept Kerry awake at night.

John sat on the hard earth and stretched out his legs. "Your parents must have had a good reason for their secrecy. Perhaps another geologist was on their trail.''

Kerry had to smile, even though it hurt her dry lips to do so. "Watch out. You're starting to sound like a deputy sheriff. Next thing you'll be suggesting foul play in my parents' deaths.''

She caught her breath. "You *are,* aren't you?''

"The circumstances have never made sense to me."

Anxiety made her throat even drier. She longed to ask John for a drink but didn't dare admit her canteen was empty. "Why?"

"They were experienced backpackers, traveling well equipped and in a pair."

No! Her stomach and her mind rebelled at what he was suggesting. "My father broke his leg and was unable to keep moving. Mother wouldn't leave him alone...."

"Even so, they should have been able to survive the week it took for someone to come looking for them."

"If this is where he was injured, they wouldn't have had any water," Kerry said. Without hydration, a person resting in the shade could expect to survive two days, maximum, in the desert.

"True enough. But they weren't novices. Your mother would have known where to look and how to conserve whatever supplies they had."

John was vocalizing thoughts she'd had a thousand times. There *were* inconsistencies in the scenario the authorities had reconstructed for the family. Both her aunt and uncle, and Kerry when she was older, had smoothed over the facts to come up with the most logical explanation for the couple's demise.

But what if something more diabolical had happened?

"When I turned eighteen, Uncle Hamilton discussed the accident in more detail with me. Apparently the autopsy report stated that there were contusions to my father's head. The assumption was that the injuries occurred in the same fall that broke his leg.''

"Maybe, Kerry. But was the fall an accident? The canyon drops suddenly, yes, but isn't it possible that he might have been pushed? Though why wouldn't he have pushed your mother over too?''

"Anyone who knew my mother would realize that by disabling her husband they disabled her. She would never leave him. But who could be so vicious?''

"You were so young. Do you remember any of the people your parents worked with?''

Kerry's mind raced with possibilities. She really couldn't recall much. Then an obvious suspect occurred to her. "Well, there would have been the pilot who was flying the helicopter when they first spotted the unusual formation. They had him circle the area twice so they would recognize it when they came back on foot.''

"Do you know who the pilot was?''

Something in her memory teased her. Kerry frowned with frustration. "I think I *did*, but darned if I can remember his name or even what he looked like.''

"You were only five.''

Yeah. But this was important. "If the pilot thought my parents were after something valuable, he might have followed them on foot into the mountains. Perhaps he caught up to them at this very spot and fought with my father. Either accidentally, or on purpose, he pushed my father into the canyon, and my father fell onto the ledge.''

Kerry realized, sickeningly, that they were talking about manslaughter at a minimum. Possibly even murder. She couldn't stop herself from envisioning what might have happened. To completely disable her father and mother, this stranger would have only had to empty their canteens and take away their food. That would leave them virtually helpless.

What kind of person was capable of such cruelty?

"I can't believe it, John. But if it's true, then we may be on a wild-goose chase. Because if the stranger *did* know what he was looking for, perhaps he found it.''

That thought brought her to a new conclusion. One in all her imaginings she had never before contemplated.

When she and John reached the end of the trail, they might well discover…nothing.

"THAT's a distinct possibility," John admitted. "But there are others. Perhaps there was no other man, no struggle, no homicide.''

"I wish that was true," Kerry said. "But our theory explains so much that didn't make sense before.''

"Agreed. But that doesn't guarantee that whoever hurt your parents found success himself. Even assuming he knew what he was looking for, he may never have found the access to Black Valley.''

John shifted uncomfortably on the hard rock. The more he weighed the alternatives, the more uneasy he became. Perhaps he and Kerry were complicating the situation with their imaginings. But he didn't think so. Sometimes in his job, he got a gut feeling about a specific case. That a certain person was guilty, or lying, or hiding something. Generally, when he got one of those hunches, it turned out to be right.

And he was having one right now.

It's this spot that is doing it to me. He stood on his feet shakily, then rubbed a hand over his face. Kerry's parents had died here. Were their spirits trying to reach him? Trying to make him understand what had happened?

Oh, God, he was thinking like his grandfather. This was insane. And yet, he couldn't deny that the location held an aura. Kerry seemed to feel it, too. She was rubbing a rock she'd picked up from the ground like a talisman.

''What are the possibilities with that last theory of yours?'' she asked quietly.

''Well. The stranger could have given up and gone home. Or he might have died trying to find the secret passageway.''

''So we shouldn't give up.''

''Were you, even for one minute, considering it?''

''Not really. Although…''

Kerry sighed, and he thought how tired she looked.

For the first time he was flooded with intense worry. The natural obstacles of the desert he could cope with. But what if there were other dangers he hadn't thought of?

"I suppose we should consider the possibility that it wasn't Evan in that helicopter, after all," he said.

Kerry's eyes rounded solemnly. "You mean the man who killed my parents?"

"It's possible. Maybe he's a friend of the family or still an employee at the Land Bureau who heard about your plans and got suspicious about where you were going and what you might be searching for." John scanned the blue, cloudless sky. All was quiet and calm.

Despite the apparent peace, he felt anxious and restless. "Let's get moving."

Kerry seemed a little shaky as she pulled herself to her feet, but true to form, she ignored his proffered hand.

"The switchbacks are going to start soon. We'll be gaining a lot of elevation in a very short period of time. Make sure you drink lots." He'd filled both their canteens this morning, and his was still half full. "Don't worry about conserving any of your water. You're going to need every drop today."

She was twisting her hair into her usual ponytail, so he couldn't see her face. But she nodded.

"Why don't you keep leading," she told him. "We need to get past this stretch before the sun is too high."

She was right. They had no time to lose, what with their argument this morning, then spotting those horses and finally the long discussion. Still, he wished the path was wider so they could walk abreast. He hated having her out of his sight, even though all he had to do was turn his head to see her.

John felt the heat bearing down on him as he set a pace somewhat more relaxed than earlier that morning. One worry nagged him. Kerry had to be tired if she wasn't pushing to lead anymore.

Pausing at a dried-up creek, he made an offer. "If you want, we could take a break. I could probably find some water here with a little digging."

Kerry examined the dried creek bed with obvious skepticism. "No. Let's keep going."

"Fine." Stubborn woman. He should have known better than to make the offer. Adjusting the pack higher on his back, John picked up the trail on the other side of the old creek.

Although he couldn't see her, with every step his thoughts were on the woman behind him. Their argument from that morning played in his brain like an obnoxious advertising jingle. *You're just making excuses, John. You're just making excuses.*

If only she knew how he really felt. How totally obsessed he was with her. How desperately he wanted her, now and always.

He'd learned something on this trip, all right. Getting over Kerry, resisting Kerry—these things were impossible. Being her friend, a man on the sidelines of her life, wouldn't work. Especially not now, after they'd made love.

How could he go back to his old life knowing all this? He still visited her aunt and uncle from time to time, still kept up his friendship with Zach and his twin brother, Zane. Even if he tried not to, he'd occasionally see Kerry, and he'd certainly hear about her from her family.

But what option did he have?

The answer seemed obvious. He had to leave this part of Nevada and make a new life for himself.

When they returned to so-called civilization, he would resign from his job and start looking for a new one. Maybe he'd try a different state, New Mexico or Texas. Someplace far away where he wouldn't be tempted to try to see Kerry again.

It was the right decision, yet John didn't find the peace he yearned for. Behind him, he listened intently for the sounds of Kerry gamely plodding on. He was tempted to tell her about his new plans, if only to truly commit himself to them.

But he knew he couldn't. Kerry would argue against him leaving, out of kindness, if nothing else. Deep down she'd be relieved that he'd taken the choice out of her hands.

They were well into the switchback turns. The path—really nothing more than a trail made by coyotes and rabbits—wove across the rock face in long, almost horizontal zigzags.

It was a daunting stretch, made worse now that the

sun was higher, hotter. John pulled on his water bottle. The liquid slid down his throat, seeming to evaporate before it even hit his stomach. He wiped his mouth then turned back.

Kerry was still moving, head lowered, breath coming in rapid huffs.

"You okay?"

She didn't raise her head, just nodded and kept putting one foot in front of the other. He understood the state of exhaustion she'd reached. You didn't dare waste any oxygen on speaking; you didn't risk stopping in case you couldn't get yourself going again.

John hesitated, wondering if he dared suggest again that they take a break. But where? They were totally exposed to the sun on this aspect of the mountain. A better plan was to push on as long as they could.

"Hungry?" he asked.

"Not really."

"Okay." They'd keep traveling, he decided. As long as they were standing, they might as well keep closing in on their goal.

KERRY DIDN'T feel hungry, she was too hot and thirsty, but she knew she needed nourishment. Her limbs were shaky, and she felt light-headed. That could've been the heat, though.

She kept picturing the breakfast she'd wasted, especially the tea she'd so scornfully thrown to the flames. She'd give anything now for a cup of liquid of any type.

Probably she should admit her stupidity to John, but with every step, that became harder to do. She'd already made more than her share of mistakes. She didn't want to be the one to slow them down again.

And so she kept forcing her legs to take one step after another, pausing every few minutes to scan the sky for signs of that helicopter. She and John were so exposed on this part of the trail—no trees, not even any big boulders to hide behind.

All she had to do was push herself a few hours more. Tonight John would find water, catch them something for dinner. If she could just hang on for a little while longer.

Ahead of her, John continued to conquer the mountain like a relentless machine, setting a pace that was slow but steady. He never wavered or stumbled, never needed to stop to catch his breath. His long legs covered the ground with an ease she envied.

They'd been tackling the switchbacks for about an hour. She honestly didn't know how much longer she could force herself to go on. It had to be noon—the sun was beating right overhead. But John made no further mention of taking a break. Perhaps he intended to travel through the heat of the afternoon to make up for the time they'd lost earlier.

Kerry fixed her attention on the ground in front of her. While her body functioned on autopilot, her mind wandered.

She held out her hand. The first thing she felt was the coldness, the film of condensation on the exterior of the tall glass. She brought it to her lips, felt the cool liquid tease the skin of her top lip. As she tipped the glass, a chunk of ice fell forward. Water splashed her face. Don't waste it! She opened her mouth as wide as it would go, and the clear springwater flooded her throat. Ah…

"Ah!" She felt a rock give way under her boot and pitched forward unexpectedly.

"Kerry!" John sprinted and helped her to her feet.

"Sorry. I tripped." She could hardly get the words out of her parched mouth. John's canteen hung from his back. All she had to do was ask….

"We've hit the wall. Literally, I'm afraid."

She lifted her head to see what he was talking about. Twenty yards ahead, the mountain rose in castellated formation. She could spot no break in the horizontal layers of limestone, dolomite and quartzite.

"Don't tell me we have to walk around this." She could barely keep steady on her feet. Every muscle in her body ached, and she was so hot. Standing, she could feel the sweat pool between her shirt and her skin.

After a drink of water, she most longed for a cool shower. Where was a good afternoon thunderstorm when you really needed it?

"We can't walk around this." John, apparently, was oblivious to the heat. No sweat glittered on his brow or anywhere else. "The valley we're looking for is just beyond here." He slapped the side of the mountain. "There's got to be a way…."

Normally, Kerry would have been game to the challenge in John's voice. Now, though, she couldn't summon even the vaguest enthusiasm. In fact, she couldn't manage a response of any type. Her tongue felt glued to the roof of her mouth, and her head suddenly seemed too heavy for her body. Feeling as if the earth had tilted crazily, she put a hand to the rock wall of the mountain for balance.

''If only I could remember what my grandfather told me. I was hoping that once I got here, his exact words would come back. But...''

John was talking. She really ought to answer him. But it was hard to hear him over the buzzing. Was it horseflies? She tried to look for them, but her head felt so awkward and heavy. And she couldn't see anything anyway. Nothing except these annoying black dots...

CHAPTER ELEVEN

KERRY WAS FAINTING. John rushed to catch her before she hit the ground. Hell, he thought she seemed tired. Why hadn't she told him she needed to stop?

Stupid question. Because she was Kerry. And he was at fault because he'd pushed too hard. What an idiot his was. He took the straw that led from her pack and held it to her lips, noticing how dry and cracked they were. Hadn't she been drinking?

Suspicious, he dug into her pack and found the canteen. Empty. He swore. How long had she been without water? Quickly, he popped open the lid on his canteen and splashed liquid on her face. When her eyes finally opened, he poured some of the moisture into her mouth.

She moaned as the liquid splashed down her throat and over her chin.

"Here. Drink some more." Crouching beside her, he did his best to shade her from the sun as she drank steadily for several seconds.

"Thanks, John."

He pushed the canteen at her. "More." Why hadn't he noticed she was dehydrated? Thinking over the last several hours, he could pinpoint the signs.

Kerry capped the canteen, then wiped her lips. "That was so good."

"What happened to your water?"

Her gaze shifted to his left. "I used it to wash this morning. Then I... Well, then we argued, and I forgot to ask you where to fill it before we started."

"You mean you've been out of water from the very beginning of the day?" He thought of the way she'd tossed her breakfast on the fire. She hadn't had anything to eat or drink since last night.

"No wonder you fainted. Damn it, Kerry, why didn't you tell me?" He asked the question already knowing the answer. And it made him furious.

"Asking for help doesn't make you weak, you know," he said. "Especially when you're asking a friend."

Kerry's eyebrows shot up. "Friend?"

He hated everything that was implied in that one-word question of hers. She thought he'd let her down by not happily playing the role of her new lover. Why couldn't she see that it was *her* happiness he cared about more than his own?

"You don't trust me to take care of you."

She sighed. "That's all I've ever been, isn't it? Someone to look after." She pushed herself onto her feet.

"Would you sit down? You need to rest."

"No. What we need is to find the passageway into the valley."

"Plenty of time for that."

"No, there isn't. John, I know it was foolish of me not to tell you I was out of water. But I'm okay now. Let's keep moving."

Her color was returning, but he could tell she was still a little dizzy. And water remained a problem. His supply was almost depleted. In this heat, what was left wouldn't last long. And he had no idea where to find more. This wasn't familiar territory, and as he and Kerry had already discussed, her father's map was short on more than one significant detail.

He'd have to keep an eye out, he decided. Surely, something would turn up.

And just as he thought that, Kerry screamed.

"Oh, John! God, what is it?"

She plowed into his chest, and he pushed her behind him. Muscles tensed, he reached for his knife.

Kerry gave a shaky laugh. "You won't need that. It's already dead."

Then he saw what had given her the fright. A partial skeleton, including the skull and backbone, was wedged between a couple of rocks to their left.

"It's human, isn't it?" Kerry asked.

"Oh, yeah." He wasn't a medical examiner or anything, but these remains were definitely human. He wondered what had happened to this unfortunate soul. And whether his arms and legs had been torn from his body before or after death.

"Oh, God." Kerry still had her hands on his chest, transfixed by the moronic grin of the sun-bleached bones. "How long do you think this has been here?"

"A very long time."

"That's what I thought."

The shock seemed to leach out what little color Kerry had. Even the denim blue of her eyes seemed to fade.

He pushed gently on her shoulders. "Sit. Take a few deep breaths."

Predictably, she ignored his suggestion. "Do you figure anyone has seen this...besides us?"

"Well, this isn't exactly a popular backpacking trail. Other than animals, we're probably the only company this poor guy has seen since he ran into trouble."

"I'd like to feel sorry for him," Kerry said. "But if he's the one who hurt my parents..."

That had been John's first thought, even though he'd considered it far-fetched. Still, given the remote location, it wasn't impossible that this skeleton had sat here for over twenty years, unseen by another human.

"It fits, doesn't it?" Kerry speculated. "You said yourself it was possible that the stranger who killed my parents might have perished when he wasn't able to find the passageway to the valley. Now we've discovered human remains in the very spot where the passageway should have been."

"I know. It's eerie."

Kerry took a deep breath, then examined the human bones closely. After a few moments, she turned to him. "John, maybe Black Valley truly is cursed."

His logical side wanted to discount the idea. But his grandfather's blood wouldn't let him. First Kerry's parents had died. Now this man. Then there was Kerry's dream to consider. His grandfather thought dreams were more important than anything that happened when a person was awake.

If it was just him, John had no doubt what he'd do. But Kerry's safety was more important than his curiosity. And she was more physically fragile right now than she would ever admit.

"Maybe we *should* turn back."

"No way, John. I'm not saying we need to turn back. Just that we have to be careful."

"I'd love to be careful. But you don't know the meaning of the word."

She did look abashed, but her words were defiant, as usual. "We can't leave now. Forget about the passageway and the rock formations for a minute. Don't you think we should search the area for the rest of this guy? It looks as if his body parts may have been dragged away by animals."

"Yes. And there's other evidence to consider. His clothes might've disintegrated over twenty-five years, but some fragments should've remained. Rubber soles on his shoes, leather from a belt—"

"Or a wallet."

He nodded. "Exactly. But finding that stuff is going to take time." He glanced at the sky. "Which we don't have a lot of. It's probably close to two in the afternoon now." And they were almost out of water.

He didn't mention this last worry because Kerry might still be dehydrated, and he didn't want her not to drink if she was thirsty. He'd find more water. He *had* to.

"Maybe we can search for the remains while we look for the passageway." Kerry circled the morbid skeleton, then began working her way west.

John followed. It might be faster to split up and cover more territory, but he wasn't letting her out of his sight.

In a methodical fashion, they scoured the area out from the remains in ever broadening swathes. Half an hour passed before he noticed one end of a femur protruding from a small gap in the rocks.

"This looks like it could be an abandoned coyote den." On hands and knees, he cautiously explored. Sure enough, he found old remains of small mammals. But some of the gnawed bones were larger. Human, he suspected.

He hauled out what he could but was unable to reach into the far corners of the den.

Kerry observed his predicament. "Let me get a stick."

A minute later she was back with a twisted branch from a dead tree.

"Let me try. My arms are thinner." In fact, she was able to get her entire upper body into the opening.

Watching Kerry half-disappear into the earth was

a freaky experience. John placed a hand on her hip. "That's far enough."

Some excited mumbling came from inside the cave. He felt her struggle to go in deeper.

"That's enough," he repeated, louder. He was sure the cave had been abandoned by whatever creature had filled it with old bones, but that didn't mean other dangers weren't lurking. He tugged on Kerry's legs, trying to pull her out.

"What are you doing?"

"Kerry, have you considered that a snake or a scorpion could be curled up in there for a nice afternoon nap?"

"Oh." She squirmed out, her expression queasy. "I hadn't thought of that." He could see her backbone straighten as she regained her resolve. "But something else is in there. I could feel it with the stick. I have to go in farther."

"Let me do it."

"John, you're too big." She glanced at his shoulders and put her hand on one. Before he could say a word, she ducked into the small opening. This time the den swallowed her up to her knees. John kept a firm hold on her booted feet, all the while thinking that a venomous bite was just what they needed right now.

He was still anticipating a piercing scream of pain when she emerged, her face red but smiling. "Look what I found!"

In her hand she held a tattered leather wallet.

"Hot damn. I don't believe it."

It was dirty but not in bad shape otherwise. He watched as Kerry flipped to a compartment containing several credit cards, a driver's license...*a pilot's license.*

"Brian Henderson," Kerry read aloud.

John glanced at the ID picture of a man in his forties with dark hair and a thick, unkempt mustache. He'd be able to perform a full check into the man's background at the office. For now, however, the presence of a pilot's license was pretty strong circumstantial evidence that this man had indeed known Kerry's parents.

John tried to take the wallet from Kerry—he'd hand it in at the sheriff's office as evidence—but she refused to let go. She stared at the photo ID, a frown tugging at the corners of her mouth. John felt a foreboding shiver as he guessed at her fascination.

"What is it?" he asked. "Do you know this guy?"

SHE'D BEEN only five at the time, but Kerry was certain she remembered the man in the photograph. She'd called him Uncle Brian, and he had called her a rock fiend like her parents.

"Empty your pockets of all those stones before you get on my helicopter," he'd warned. He'd probably been teasing. At the time she'd honestly believed the rock collection she had stuffed into every available pocket of her overalls might keep the helicopter from taking off into the sky.

And so she'd dumped them all into the back seat of her parents' car.

"He took me flying with them one time," she said slowly, as the memory came to her. Lord, how could she have forgotten her first helicopter ride? But she had. Until she'd seen that picture of Brian—*Uncle Brian*—it had totally skipped her mind.

Her parents' death, coming shortly thereafter, must have totally eclipsed the event.

"Not *the* time?" John asked. "When they spotted Black Valley?"

Surely not. Or was it possible? She'd always had such a vivid recollection of her parents asking the pilot to circle to the rock formation they'd spotted, but she'd never guessed it was because she'd been there and heard them make the request.

"I was there." She still found it difficult to believe. "I was in the helicopter that day. I remember how excited they both were, and Dad passed me the binoculars, but I couldn't get them to work. I didn't see anything."

Her mom and dad had been so thrilled, though. Almost as soon as they were on land, they began planning a return trip to the desert—on foot this time. It must have been that night when Kerry had overheard her parents' conversation. Her mother saying she'd like to bring Kerry along on the expedition; her father insisting the trip would be too dangerous.

Strange how easily the pieces fell together. All

she'd needed was that one memory prod, that picture of Uncle Brian.

"He was a family friend," she told John. "I hate to think he could have done such an evil thing."

"I guess we can't understand without knowing what they saw in that valley."

Kerry's curiosity was unbearable. She needed to get into Black Valley and find out what, exactly, had caused all this madness.

She couldn't imagine anything that could be worth her parents' lives.

"If we're right about what happened it seems so unfair. Brian Henderson got away with murder."

"If Henderson was responsible for what happened to your parents, I wouldn't say he went unpunished. Nature appears to have taken her own retribution."

His comment reminded her of her dream. "The curse," she whispered softly.

"Maybe so." John reached for her hand, and she squeezed his tightly, glad for the human connection.

She flipped the wallet shut and let John stuff it into his back pocket. Feeling vaguely uneasy, she stepped around the pile of bones John had unearthed from the cave. "Do you think we should bury Brian Henderson's remains?"

"How? The ground is nothing but rock. Don't worry. I'll send out an official search party when we get back. They'll take care of what's left of Brian Henderson. Inform any living relatives of his death. I imagine there'll be an inquest, as well."

Kerry wondered what an inquest would accomplish after so many years had passed. Forensics would probably determine the cause and approximate date of Henderson's death. But even if it turned out Henderson died within days or weeks of her parents, it was highly unlikely they'd find evidence to link Henderson to their deaths.

Not that it mattered. Henderson was dead. And it wasn't hard to imagine his fate had been meted out by a power Kerry had never believed in before.

These last few days, though, she'd allowed herself to become obsessed by native American legends, the possibility of ancient curses and communication with the dead through dreams. Anyone but John would be thinking she was losing her mind.

But John understood.

She dropped her gaze to his hand, entwined with hers. Nothing in her life had felt as real or as important as these days in the desert with John. Last night they'd made love for the first time. She'd told John she loved him. She'd said the words without thinking, without analyzing. She'd spoken from the heart.

But did she really love him? The way a woman loved a man she wanted to spend the rest of her life with?

She was used to assessing her feelings from twenty different angles, so the simplicity, the ease with which the answer came to her was amazing.

Yes.

CHAPTER TWELVE

KERRY hadn't spoken in minutes. The way she was looking at him, John was pretty sure she wasn't thinking about Brian Henderson anymore.

She was thinking about *him,* and the expression on her face might have sent John to the moon if he hadn't known better than to put his faith in fleeting fantasies.

A plan of action was needed, but John found his cognitive powers paralyzed. How could a man think when Kerry gazed at him, her blue eyes putting the washed-out sky to shame. Kissing her suddenly seemed like the best idea in the world. But for him, it also happened to be one of the more dangerous.

"We have to get moving," he reminded her. "We need to find water before nightfall."

"You're right," she agreed, and yet she didn't move or shift her gaze. And he, fool that he was, couldn't seem to break the spell that held them together, either.

He threw out the only word that could protect him, a talisman to ward off love. "Evan. Have you been missing him at all?"

"Oh, John." Kerry's soft sigh spoke of amused

exasperation. "I gave Evan two years of my time. The way I'm feeling right now, that was about one year and ten months too long."

Are you sure? He'd asked the question before, and didn't see the point in raising it again. For some reason Kerry had become infatuated with him. Right now wasn't the time to appeal to her reason.

And maybe it wasn't the right time to appeal to his, either.

He'd never considered Kerry the perfect woman, but he knew she was perfect for him. Just imagining the two of them together was a heady, exhilarating ride. For a wild moment he envisioned her by his side, riding horses just like in the old days, going camping on weekends, making dinner together at home, then cuddling in front of the TV for a movie.

An unpretentious, simple life, perhaps, but it was all he wanted—if he could have Kerry.

But now he added in dashes of reality to give the real picture. A snide comment about interracial relationships from someone in the lineup to buy a movie ticket; the looks of resignation and disappointment on the faces of Kerry's relatives on their wedding day. And worse, in a year or two, a new child born into the world, not knowing where he truly belonged.

Idiot. John branded himself and his dreams with the only possible description.

Forget the world he'd glimpsed in Kerry's eyes. Focus on the task before them. It wasn't as if he didn't have serious enough issues to think about.

Curiosity made him want to keep searching for the passageway to the valley. Caution warned him they couldn't go much longer without finding water. He took a few steps back from Kerry, and as she followed, he noticed how pronounced her limp had become. Clearly, she was exhausted.

Water. Where could he find it? Probably in the valley, but they still had no idea how to get there, or even if a passage was possible.

He thought of the dried creek they'd encountered on the way up. If only he'd known then that Kerry's canteen was empty. Digging for water would have taken only a few minutes.

He had a dilemma. Keep going, and hope he ran across a fresh supply? Or descend that grueling series of switchbacks and fill up at the creek? The second option could end up eating an hour, possibly two. But if he didn't go back and didn't find water today or later this evening...

John realized he had only one choice.

He scanned the surroundings for a sheltered spot that would offer a little shade, a comfortable place to rest. When he found it, he knew the hardest part would be convincing Kerry she should stay here and wait while he went for water.

WITH EVERY FIBER of her being, Kerry tried to argue against John's plan. She didn't want them to be separated. It wasn't fair for him to make the trek down the mountain on his own. Especially when the water shortage was her fault.

She wanted to argue, but she was too tired. This last half hour, she'd been fueled by willpower and nothing else. She'd used her reserves, and then some.

The truth was, if she tried to accompany John, she'd only slow him down.

"Okay," she conceded, collapsing into the shade. "You go ahead and find the water. I'll stay put."

"You promise you won't move? You won't try to find the passageway on your own?"

Oh, it was an intriguing possibility. But one she was physically incapable of following through on. "Don't worry about me. I'll just order some room service and catch a few winks."

Poor John's brow creased with worry.

"Just joking," she assured him. "I promise I'm not hallucinating or anything." She tossed him her canteen. "You'll want to fill this up, I assume."

He caught the nylon bag neatly, then rummaged in the pack for some food. "Here." He dropped several packets of dried provisions at her feet. "Make sure you eat. And drink the rest of this water before I go."

He held out his canteen.

God, she wanted that water! But she shook her head firmly. "No way, John. I need you to come back alive."

Saying the words out loud put the entire situation into perspective. They truly were in a life-or-death situation. Three people had already died trying to make it past this mountain. If John didn't find water soon enough, if he didn't make his way back in time, she would die, too. And possibly John, as well.

Wouldn't that make an ironic ending to her parents' story? Twenty-five years after their untimely death, their only daughter succumbed to the same fate.

"John, I got you into this mess. I'm sorry. If I hadn't been so stubborn, I could have flagged that helicopter down. They would have been able to land at a lower elevation and we could've scrambled to meet them. Right now you'd be drinking a beer and ordering a steak instead of—"

John put his hand to her mouth. "First, Kerry, I *want* to be here. Okay? And second, this isn't your fault. I should have checked both canteens before we started this morning."

Oh, she loved him for trying to take the blame.

"Will you be back before dark?"

"Well before," he promised. John adjusted the straps on her pack before slipping them over his shoulders. He started to leave, then abruptly turned back. Dipping down to his knees, he brought his face level with hers and kissed her gently on the mouth.

"Please be here when I get back."

With her eyes she drank in every familiar, strong, beautiful detail of his face. Gently, she touched her hand to his cheek. "Please *get* back."

KERRY'S EXHAUSTION pulled her under quickly, but her sleep was fitful and uncomfortable, and filled with far too many images of sparkling, refreshing beverages that disappeared the moment she reached out her hand or parted her lips.

In her brief waking periods, she wondered how John was faring. She imagined him descending the terrain they'd covered that morning, trying to time his progress to the movements of the shadows on the rock in front of her. Without her to hold him up, he'd be faster, for sure. But he had twice the distance to cover, plus she had to factor in some time for him to find water.

She noted the sun's position relative to the mountain cornice currently offering her shade, then closed her eyes. She slipped into her dream world, finding herself at the edge of the ocean, mesmerized by the constant lapping of lazy waves.

She longed to go swimming, to throw herself into the cool, clean water, to immerse her hot, sticky body and emerge fresh and whole. She wanted to feel her hair streaming through the water behind her, her entire body buoyed by the waves and the salt.

Ah… She sighed and dreamed on, not fully asleep, but anxious to stay in this fantasyland as long as possible. A sensation of scorching heat on her hand brought her out of the trancelike state.

She opened her eyes to see a ribbon of sunlight cutting across her body. The sun had moved, and with it the shade. Though she crawled back several feet, she found little relief. Even out of direct sunlight, the heat was stifling. She did her best to forget about oceans and cool breezes and ice-cold beer.

Her stomach rumbled, reminding her that she hadn't eaten much. With shaking hands she gathered the provisions John had left her. The dried meat and fruit had never looked less appetizing, but she forced herself to open a packet and take a bite.

On her parched tongue, the food felt like dirt. She chewed and chewed, forever, it seemed, before finally forcing herself to swallow. Each granule nearly choked her as it traveled down her throat.

Slowly, methodically, she gnawed her way through the entire package of dried apple and strawberry. When she'd finished, she was even more desperate for water than before.

How much longer would John be? She didn't think she could stand any more of this waiting.

Maybe she could look around a little. She wouldn't go far, and she'd keep the cornice in sight.

As she pulled herself up, her legs started shaking, and her bad foot ached. She could feel every one of the bruises she'd sustained during her tumble two days ago.

Two days only. It was hard to believe her fall had happened so recently. So much had occurred in the space of forty-eight hours. Really, her entire life had been stood on end.

John. She was going to have to change his mind about their future. But she didn't know how. She couldn't change her skin color or his. More to the point, she didn't want to.

What she felt for him was love. Not just the longing for a family and children, which had been behind her feelings for Evan. But a wholehearted passion for a man whose simple presence at her side made everything in the world suddenly make sense. Given the chance, she'd link her life to John's without any hesitation.

If they could love each other for what they were, what did it matter if others disapproved? She knew her family wouldn't. John was wrong about them, wrong about their attitudes. Somehow she had to prove that to him, as well.

Kerry rolled the rest of her food into her sleeping bag and tucked the bundle under a rock in case a breeze stirred up. If only one would! At this point, even a desert rainstorm would be a welcome respite from the hot stillness.

As she left her shelter, she felt an annoying glimmer of guilt. *You won't try to find the passageway without me?* She'd promised she wouldn't. But she was so bored, and a little action would take her mind off the heat and the waiting.

She wouldn't go far, she reasoned, and John wouldn't mind as long as she was careful. If she remained here doing nothing, she ran the risk of going insane. And it *was* possible she might find something useful.

But she'd taken just one step from behind the rocky

cornice when she spotted a familiar tan-colored creature. The coyote's presence stopped her in her tracks.

"What are you doing here?"

The creature was close enough that she could follow the movement of his eyes as he looked at her, then through her.

Kerry stared at the animal for several minutes, trying to decide how frightened she should be. He didn't look vicious. If this was their trickster, maybe he was here for a purpose. To show them they were on the right path?

Or to keep her pinned in this spot until John returned?

"You little devil..." As soon as she made the comment, she realized how ridiculous it was. This poor animal was probably curious. Or maybe, like her, he was so hot he'd decided to sit down for a rest.

But, as long as he stayed where he was, she couldn't move. She didn't dare. For as innocent as the coyote's presence had been until now, she wasn't taking any chances of getting attacked. If it came down to a battle between the two of them, she feared she wouldn't be the one to emerge on the top of the food chain.

Resigned, Kerry sank to the ground. After a while her head grew heavy again, and she began to daydream. As they'd done so many times these past few days, her thoughts turned to that time she and John had disappeared in the mountains. Her poor aunt.

Later, she'd told Kerry how terribly afraid she'd been that night.

ELEANOR DUMAS had decided to check on her niece—who'd gone to bed early with a sore tummy—at eight o'clock. That was when she found the pillows under the covers where a little eight-year-old girl should have been.

Stilling the urge to scream in panic, Eleanor instead yelled for her children. "Zach. Zane. Melinda." They came at a run, but none of them had a clue where Kerry was. Eleanor sent Zach to the barns to tell Hamilton. Zane was commissioned to search Kerry's favorite outdoor haunts. Melinda went through every nook and cranny in the house.

After fifteen minutes, Eleanor started phoning neighbors. It wasn't until almost nine that Hamilton suggested they call their foreman.

Only the Eagles didn't have a phone. So Hamilton had to drive. By the time he arrived at the old mountain shack, the sun had long dipped past the hills to the west. His foreman came to the door, closing it firmly behind him so they could speak in privacy on the front porch.

After hearing the tale, Mr. Eagle went inside to talk to his son. Seconds later, he was back at the door, enflamed.

"Johnny's missing, too. It must've been—" He'd choked back the rest of his thought and bent down. He seemed to be counting the floorboards of the porch. Hamilton wondered if the man had lost his senses.

But suddenly the foreman bent low and pried one of the boards loose. He reached his hand underneath the hollow space and retrieved a rifle.

"We'll take the dog," he said, opening the door again—just a crack—and whistling. Out bounded a rangy black mutt.

"Come on, Friday," the foreman said. "Find Johnny for us."

JOHN WAS BACK with the water sooner than he'd hoped. He'd found the dried-up creek and had only needed to dig a few inches before he'd hit water. Both canteens were full, which should buy them another twenty-four hours.

With that worry off his mind, his thoughts focused, quite naturally, on the other subject of concern. Kerry.

He hoped he'd find her where he'd left her, but it wasn't in Kerry's nature to stay put for too long, especially when adventure was calling. And man, adventure was sure calling them today.

First catching sight of those wild horses, then stumbling over Brian Henderson's remains and finally Kerry fainting. All that action, and what did his thoughts keep wanting to dwell on? That mad moment when Kerry had been holding his hand and begging him with her eyes to kiss her.

Did she have any idea how crazy she was making him?

His willpower was only so strong.

John had to keep reminding himself why it was important to resist. It didn't matter how he felt about Kerry or how Kerry felt about him. Even if she truly did care about him, they had no business planning a future together. He had to put Kerry's best interests—and those of any future children—ahead of his own.

He rounded the last ninety-degree turn and hurried toward the spot where he'd left her. The sun was at his back, a reminder of the hours they'd squandered. Please, God, let Kerry be waiting for him. Surely she wouldn't be bullheaded enough to take off on her own without water.

He started to run.

The heat from the sun wrapped around his limbs and his face like hot dry cloths. Breathing became an effort as the heat sucked out his instinct for survival.

Kerry. He used her name to goad himself until finally he saw the jut in the mountain where he'd settled her for the wait. The sight gave him fresh motivation. He slugged back some water, which seemed to turn instantly into perspiration on his forehead and back.

Until now, he'd dealt quite well with the demands of the desert sun. But most of the time he'd been traveling at Kerry's slower pace. Truthfully, he may have pushed himself a little too hard these past few hours.

He was there. Or almost. Just twenty more yards. But suddenly his legs threatened to give out on him.

He leaned against the ubiquitous mountain and shielded his eyes.

"Kerry?" One of the smaller, tan-colored rocks shifted right before his eyes. Was he out of his mind?

"Kerry?"

"I'm here, John."

Her voice came faintly from behind the rocks where he'd left her in the shade. Thank goodness! But why wasn't she coming to meet him?

The pile of rocks ahead of him seemed to move again. This time a shape emerged, and within that shape, a pair of wild amber eyes.

It was a coyote. Blocking the entrance to Kerry's hiding place.

John swore, reached for his knife, then paused.

Was this just a coyote? Or was it his and Kerry's coyote? Their trickster?

"Are you okay?" he called.

"Fine. But I'm getting a little tired of waiting for that carnivore to make up his mind whether I'm going to be appetizer or dessert."

"Neither. Come on, Kerry. He's our mascot, remember? He's not going to hurt you." It *was* strange, though, to see a coyote in the full heat of day and obviously not at all wary of humans.

"Did you happen to notice the fangs on our mascot?"

He laughed, then forced his aching legs to carry him forward. Slowly and cautiously, he closed in on the wild animal, making sure he left the coyote an open escape route if he chose to run.

"What're you doing here, buddy?" he asked gently, automatically assuming a partially crouched, hunting position.

The coyote tilted his head in a gesture that reminded John of his old dog, Friday.

"You don't want to hurt us, do you? Are you here to help?" John kept his voice soft, his gaze lowered. Although he was certain the animal posed no threat to either him or Kerry, he didn't want his behavior to challenge the creature in any way.

It was a most bizarre circumstance. John's western orientation told him this was a wild animal, with no extra powers or abilities beyond those of any other creature of the desert. But the newly wakened native part of his soul had recognized something in that brief glance into the coyote's eyes. A kinship, a sense of common purpose.

Was it just bunk? John didn't think so. He took a step forward and froze. The coyote stood, then trotted away.

John worried that he'd frightened him. But the animal didn't seem afraid. He stopped and glanced over his shoulder at John. His meaning was obvious. *Well? What's keeping you?*

"Kerry! Can you get your stuff together?" He didn't dare take his eyes off the coyote long enough to go help. Thankfully he didn't need to. Within seconds, Kerry appeared from behind a tall, jagged rock.

"Is he gone?" The sleeping bag was rolled in her hands.

"I think he wants us to follow him. Come on." He gestured with his hand as the coyote began trotting again. Kerry hurried to catch up, linking her hand around his arm.

"Grab some water," he urged, passing her a filled canteen.

"Thank you." Her eyes practically rolled into her head with bliss as she took her first long, greedy pull. While she drank, he guided her forward, making sure to keep a comfortable distance from the coyote.

So hard was he focusing on the creature—despite the distracting pleasure of having Kerry pressed next to his side—that he couldn't believe his eyes when the coyote suddenly disappeared.

"Where did he go?" Kerry stumbled, then halted.

"I have no idea." He let go of Kerry to investigate. There were limits to his belief in the ancient world of spirits and magic. Physical beings couldn't vanish into thin air. John walked ahead several feet, then stopped. Instinct, too strong to be denied, told him to drop to his knees and crawl. A moment later he was glad he had.

CHAPTER THIRTEEN

KERRY CROUCHED beside John. Inches ahead of their splayed-out fingers ran a fault line in the mountain—a good four feet wide. Kerry couldn't tell how deep.

"Oh, my Lord." If John hadn't stopped when he had...

"I think we've figured out the trick behind the disappearing coyote."

"Poor thing. Do you think he hurt himself?"

John sat on his haunches, grinning.

"What's so funny?"

"A minute ago that coyote had you scared to death. Now he's a *poor thing.*" He mimicked her voice, and she slammed her fist into his shoulder.

"Watch it, buddy, or you're going down that hole after him."

"Oh, yeah?" John's playful grin faded. He glanced at the fault, shifted closer to the edge. "Oh, *yeah,*" he said softly.

Kerry examined his face suspiciously. He wasn't contemplating... He wouldn't dare...

She inched to the edge of the fault and peered down. The sun's rays were coming in at a sharp angle from the west and only illuminated the top two feet of the chasm. What lay beneath was anyone's guess. A drop of ten feet or twenty? A bottomless pit into the earth's fiery core?

"I'm checking this out." John passed her the pack after slinging his canteen over his shoulder. Feetfirst, he lowered himself into the gap.

"But, John…"

"I'll be careful."

"You'd better be." He was already down to his chest and appeared to have found some sort of foothold. She remembered the thin flashlight in her pack and retrieved it for him.

He flicked the switch and directed the steady stream of light downward. A second later, he followed that shaft of light and disappeared below the earth's surface. Kerry sat, dangling her feet into the gap, fighting the image of a wild, earth-dwelling creature grabbing her legs and dragging her into its lair.

After a few minutes she called, "You okay, John?"

"Yeah." His faint reply echoed in the rock chamber. "Got a match?"

"Don't tell me the batteries wore out already?"

"No."

He popped his head from the hole. His face was dirt-streaked, but he was smiling.

"Having fun?" She hoped he realized this little exploring junket was taking up valuable time. Still, she passed him a book of matches.

"Thanks. I just want to check how much oxygen is down here."

Before he could disappear again, she asked, "Did you find the coyote?"

"Not yet." He lowered himself out of her sight.

Several minutes passed before Kerry decided this was getting tiresome. What was so fascinating down there? She had to see for herself. She shouldered the pack, then gripping the rocky ground in front of her, she nervously eased her feet downward, searching for the same footholds that had supported John.

Unfortunately, she'd forgotten that his legs were about eight inches longer than hers. Her feet scraped the rock walls desperately, finding nothing.

"Got to get back up," she muttered. But so much of her body weight was below ground—not to mention the weight of the pack—that she wasn't strong enough to pull herself to her starting point.

Her fingers slipped, then found new purchase. *Oh, my Lord...* She shifted her weight, trying to regain lost ground. Already her muscles ached from the unaccustomed strain.

Reaching for something, *anything,* she found a rough indentation in the rock. Digging in her fingernails, she tried again to lift herself.

Instead she only slid back, losing the precious inches she'd gained and then some.

"Watch out, John! I think I'm going to—"

One minute she was clinging to the rocky edge, the next she was gripping nothing but air. She screamed on the way down and landed on something much softer than limestone.

John's back.

As she flattened him, she heard his startled exhalation. For a moment she froze in utter terror. She'd killed him.

Carefully, she shifted her weight off John and crouched by his head. No blood that she could see, but his body was trembling. The flashlight, still clutched in his hand, spilled a wavering white trail over the rock.

"Oh, John, I'm so sorry. Please be okay. Please…"

He lifted his head, and she saw he was laughing. "Jesus, Kerry."

He was fine!

"I know. I should've waited for the elevator."

He laughed again. Thank God he didn't seem to be hurt.

She scanned the dark enclosure, trying to orient herself. "What's so interesting down here, anyway?"

"Look." John scrambled up, then pointed to an opening in the rock behind her. "There's a tunnel."

And she could guess where he thought it might lead. *Can't go over it. Can't go around it…* A childhood rhyme sounded in Kerry's head. *Gotta go under it.*

"I don't like the looks of this, John."

"Do we have an option? Besides, I've checked it out. There seems to be plenty of oxygen."

He passed her the slender flashlight, and she swung it around three hundred and sixty degrees, taking stock of the situation. They were in an enclosed space just big enough for three or four people to stand. The only other exit was the narrow underground opening he'd already shown her.

Oh, boy. She wasn't claustrophobic as a rule, but this was definitely pushing the envelope.

"Do you really think we should try this?"

John confirmed her fears with a nod. "I'm pretty sure this is where our friendly little trickster meant for us to follow."

She steadied herself by gripping his shoulders. "What if he isn't a trickster? What if he's just a dumb old coyote who wasn't watching where he was going?"

"So you're voting we forget it? Try something else?"

Yeah. That was exactly what she was saying. Only…what "something else" was there? Hard as she tried, she couldn't come up with any option other than to give up and go home.

"No, I'm voting we give it a shot."

"That a girl!" He transferred the pack from her shoulders to his.

Kerry hoped she wouldn't come to regret her decision. "Any idea how far this tunnel goes?"

"None whatsoever," he said cheerfully. "But I'm betting we'll end up in Black Valley. In fact, I'm sure of it."

"Yeah, Einstein. You and the coyote." Kerry inhaled deeply. "Okay, let's go."

UNFORTUNATELY, the tunnel was too narrow for John and Kerry to travel side by side. Given the choice of leading and carrying the flashlight or following John, Kerry chose the latter.

"I don't want to meet that coyote on his way back." She rubbed her arms against the cool, dank air. An hour ago she'd longed to escape the heat. Now she craved hot sun and dry desert air. As soon as possible.

"Stay right behind me."

"Don't worry. I'm seriously contemplating tying myself to your shoelaces."

John's teeth flashed in the dark as he grinned. She could tell he was loving this.

"Be careful, Kerry." He dropped to all fours and slipped inside the opening. Kerry lost no time following. The rock was hard on her knees and the palms of her hands, but that was the least of her worries. Despite John's assurances about the oxygen, she felt anxious.

Why was he so certain this was the right path for them to take? She didn't have quite the same faith in the coyote he did. For all they knew, the creature hadn't even come down here in the first place. Or if he had, the tunnel could lead to a den or some other highly undesirable location.

Or the whole structure could collapse around them, burying them alive. Now there was a cheerful thought. Kerry concentrated on regulating her breathing, on remaining calm, on positive thoughts.

Breathe in…you're doing fine. Breathe out…this isn't so bad….

All she could make out were the soles of John's boots and the faint glow from the flashlight on the rocks ahead. Once she made the mistake of lifting her head an inch too high and almost scalped herself.

"Ow!" Her voice echoed in the small space.

John stopped moving. "You okay?"

"I guess." She rubbed her head. "Keep going." The faster they moved, the sooner this would be over. Only, what if there was no end to this tunnel? How long would it take before John would finally give up?

Maybe there was no passageway into the valley her parents had seen from the air. Maybe that was the curse, or, to put it more scientifically, the *reason* it hadn't been discovered.

Despite growing reservations, Kerry kept crawling. In sections the tunnel widened. A few times the space became so narrow, John barely pushed his shoulders through. But still he led, and she kept right behind him.

She had no idea how much time had passed when she felt a warm flow of air brush over her face. Perhaps it was just her imagination. Then she felt it again. As she drew in her next breath, the air smelled sweeter, too. John started crawling faster, and she scurried to keep up.

A flash of brightness appeared ahead. They'd made it! Each shuffle forward brought more warmth, more light. John burst through first, then held out his arms to pull her out.

They emerged in a wide-mouthed, narrow cave, not unlike where they'd started off this whole adventure.

"Well, we're alive. That's more than I counted on." She stretched tall, despite pangs of protest from her back and her knees.

"We're more than alive. We're in Black Valley." John sounded triumphant. "Come on, let's check this place out."

Together they stumbled into the sunlight, arms shielding their eyes, and found themselves in a grassy cirque.

"Wow." Kerry spun around. Mountain fortifications rose in every direction. "I feel like an ant in a very deep, narrow mixing bowl."

"A mixing bowl? Kerry, I've never been in a cathedral, but I bet even St. Paul's couldn't top this."

She knew what he meant. There was a majesty about this space, a grandeur. "Why would anyone call this *Black* Valley? It's so green." Thanks to its unique topography, the cirque was incredibly lush. Rain would collect here in the summer, snow in the winter. The high, protective mountain walls would impede evaporation, fostering the growth of abundant vegetation.

"I wonder where our coyote got to?" She felt like she owed him her thanks and maybe an apology for doubting him. Whether the animal had special powers or not, they'd never have found the underground passageway without his help.

"Hundreds of places for a coyote to hide in here. Compared to the desert, this is paradise."

"Do you think there's room for someone to land a helicopter?"

John assessed the surrounding mountains, the relatively small area of level land space. "No way."

She nodded. That explained why her parents had elected to make this journey on foot. She resisted the urge to let out a celebratory whoop. They'd found the valley, but their quest was not yet over. She retrieved the map and looked for the drawing of the brave's profile.

"We still need to find this. What direction do you think?"

John oriented himself to the sun, then consulted the map again. Finally, he pointed directly toward the west. "I think it's that way. But we'd get a better idea if we could find a lookout."

Kerry studied their surroundings. "What about that pile of rock over there?"

The debris from a small landslide had created a perch that ought to be easy enough to scramble onto. John offered her a hand.

"Game?"

"You bet."

Her foot didn't hurt, nor did she feel any hint of fatigue as she climbed the piled stones with John. They gained elevation quickly and after only a few minutes were able to turn and survey the surrounding area.

Kerry couldn't remember ever feeling more anxious. ''Do you see anything?''

''I see lots of things. This is very beautiful, Kerry. But what's that huge rock over there?''

She glanced around but saw only low-growing shrubs and thick grass punctuated by chunks of rock.

John took hold of her shoulders and directed her gaze in line with the setting sun. Following his pointed finger, she finally saw a dark slab of rock that stood out from the others.

''Oh, my Lord, John. It's a meteorite.'' She could tell, even from this distance, that the huge hunk of minerals was not of this world.

''You're saying that rock came here from outer space?''

''Exactly right. It could have been a piece of space debris, or maybe a hunk of the moon or even Mars! John, isn't this amazing?

''John?'' She realized then that he wasn't gaping with wonder at the rock the way she was. He was staring at her and smiling.

''Trust you to get so excited about a rock.''

''A rock? John, that piece of stone out there may well hold the mystery to the beginning of our solar system. No wonder my parents were so excited. This find would have made their professional reputations.''

Just as it would make hers, when she told the world what she'd found here.

"John, this even fits with your grandfather's legend. When he spoke of the fire in the heavens that showered sparks into the air—he could have been referring to a meteorite shower. When the flaming pieces fell to the earth, they could have set trees and shrubs on fire."

"Well, you're the geologist. I still say it was just a story."

Shielding the sun from her eyes with her hands, Kerry hopped with excitement as she spotted something new. "Just a story, huh? Then explain that!" She moved John over a few feet so he could see the meteorite from a different angle.

And there it was, the profile of the brave, just as her father had sketched it on the map. Proud forehead, straight nose, strong chin, all etched into the side of the large, dark boulder.

"Well, hell."

"It's difficult to believe, isn't it?" she said softly. "Like seeing one of those photos of flattened rings in farmers' fields—you're just so certain it has to be a hoax. But this is real, John. I know it."

"Hell." Kerry could hear the disbelief fading from John's voice. "The damn thing looks just the way my grandfather described it to me."

"We've got to get a closer look before it's too dark." Grabbing John's hand, she began to scramble down.

"Hey, why so fast? The rock isn't going anywhere."

"Aren't you excited? I can't believe we found it. It really exists!"

Once she hit level ground she broke out running, towing John until he took over the lead, saving her from a nasty fall when she tripped over a rock hidden by a tuft of dry grass. She was breathless by the time they stopped within a hand's reach of the largest chunk of meteorite.

The rock's deep-brown color made it obvious it couldn't have broken off from any of the surrounding mountains. Gently, Kerry brushed her fingertips over the surface. Even the texture was unique.

"Wouldn't you love to know where this has been? I wonder how long ago it crashed to earth."

John put out a hand, then hesitated. "This is kind of weird. Is it radioactive or anything?"

"No. Possibly magnetic, but touching certainly won't hurt you." She stroked her hand down the sharp angles of the profile, then began working her way around to the side. With her fingers, she explored every nook and cranny, rubbing the rock like a crystal ball.

Even a scientific mind like hers was inclined to be a little superstitious when encountering something like this. "Extraterrestrial material fallen from the heavens to earth. It makes a person wonder, doesn't it?"

Indulgently, John peered over her head, resting a hand on her shoulder. "But really, it's just a hunk of minerals, right? With all due respect to my ancestors, this stone doesn't have any special powers."

This was true, but briefly, Kerry wished that it wasn't. That if she rubbed hard enough, she'd be granted three wishes. Or even one. One would be enough. She paused her exploration when she came to a significant indentation.

"Hey, look over here."

John leaned closer to check it out.

She slipped her fingers into the concavity. The tiny hole was just over an inch in diameter. Using her baby finger, she probed the space, then gasped as her nail scraped into something that moved.

"I don't believe this." The surface felt hard and polished. Metal, shaped in a ring—wait, there were two of them. Curling her finger inward, she hooked them with her nail and brought them into the light.

"Gold wedding bands." John sounded puzzled.

Suddenly light-headed, Kerry passed him the larger ring while she took the smaller. In the fading light she read the inscription. "William and Susanna, forever. My parents, John."

"So they made it."

Kerry smiled. "Isn't it wonderful? Oh, John, they must've been so thrilled."

"But why did they leave their rings behind?"

Had her parents known they were being followed? Did they suspect they might not make it home alive? Kerry would never discover the answers to those questions, but nevertheless, she felt that the rings had been left for her to find.

She slipped her mother's band onto the fourth finger of her right hand, next to the diamond engagement ring. John still held on to the gold band that had been her father's.

"Where should I put it?" he asked.

"Slip it on, so we can't lose it. Does it fit?"

It did. Perfectly.

Kerry shivered, and John put an arm around her back. "The sun's gone down," she said, as if that explained the chill that had crawled down her back. She knew it didn't. "We need to set up camp for the night."

"Let's head back to the cave. Then I'll go get us some water. I think I spotted a likely source by that rock pile."

Kerry nodded. The routine was familiar to her. While John took care of the water, she would gather fuel for their evening fire. Tonight they would celebrate the treasure they had found.

In the morning they would have to plan the trek back to civilization. Right now, though, home, Reno, her job and Evan were the last subjects she wanted to think about.

Thirty minutes later, they were settled for the night. Their canteens were full once more, and John had started a fire. Since he couldn't hunt in the dark, they were making do with her dry provisions for dinner. Again.

Easing back against the rock wall behind her and squaring her toes to the flames of their campfire, Kerry sank into the pleasure of resting after a deeply taxing day. Even with her eyes closed, though, all she could think about was the meteorite.

"Wasn't it something, John?" As kids they would have been disappointed to have worked so hard, only to find a rock. But for Kerry there could have been no greater treasure, especially since they'd also found her parents' rings.

"You didn't take any photographs."

She'd thought about it. Been tempted. "I'm not so sure I want anyone else to know about this. I suppose that sounds crazy to you."

But the moment she and John had put her parents' rings on their respective fingers, she'd had the eeriest sensation. *This is a sacred spot.* The legend was true. And she was convinced that her parents had felt the same when they'd come upon the meteorite twenty-five years ago.

That's why they'd left their rings. As offerings of love. She felt quite confident that even if they'd completed their journey successfully, her parents would never have capitalized on what they had found.

And she wouldn't, either.

"I don't think you're crazy at all," John said. "I happen to agree with you. There's something kind of magical about that spot. I'd hate to see it turned into a tourist attraction."

Kerry rested her chin on her bent knees and regarded John's profile. The fire threw his shadow against the cave wall. Eerie how much it resembled the natural carving in the rock.

"I wonder who else has seen what we saw today."

"Many of my people have heard the legend. Probably only a few realize the stone actually exists. My grandfather, I'd guess, was one of them."

"What do you make of that brave staying to face death rather than traveling on with the rest of his tribe?"

John shrugged. "Perhaps he was stubborn? Foolish?"

She wasn't put off by John's levity. She knew that on some level he took the legend quite seriously. "The brave faced death rather than leave the land he loved. That's a powerful message, don't you think?"

John wasn't stupid. He had to see where she was leading with this. As surely as that brave belonged on this mountain, she and John were meant to be together.

Their early friendship had been portentous. Looking back, she couldn't regret any longer that they'd spent the most recent years apart. That time had allowed them to mature, to experience the world and date other people. Now, though, it was time for them to come together again. Surely John had to see it.

"I suppose that's one interpretation." It was all John said. "What about the curse? Have you decided it doesn't exist, after all?"

"We aren't home yet," she reminded him. Then

she shivered and wished she'd kept those words, and her misgivings, to herself. Exacerbating the suddenly eerie atmosphere, a coyote howled in the distance. She wondered if it was their mascot. Their trickster.

Strange how he'd led them to the underground passageway. Was it possible the animal had truly meant for them to follow him? At this point, Kerry realized, she was prepared to believe that he had.

CHAPTER FOURTEEN

KERRY'S EYELIDS were drooping when John stood beside the campfire.

"I have a surprise for you." He held out his hand.

Where did he get his energy? "Unless it's a king-size bed, I'm not interested."

"I think you will be. Come on." He bent to grasp her hand, then pulled her up.

"This better be good," she grumbled as he led her out of their cave into the night. From behind the shifting bands of clouds, she glimpsed a full moon and a bucketful of scattered stars.

John covered her shoulders with his arm, urging her along a path that apparently only he could see. After the first couple of minutes, she couldn't resist complaining again. "After the day we just had, you'd think I'd at least deserve a decent night's sleep."

"Trust me. This is going to be a real treat."

Well, right or wrong, she *did* trust him, so she kept following for at least another five minutes. Then a strange odor teased her senses. She sniffed, walked farther, then sniffed again.

"Smells like sulfur."

John picked up his pace a little, then abruptly

stopped. Kerry heard the bubbling sound of water dancing over stones. Moonlight reflected in dozens of tiny flashes in a pool to her right.

"I found this when I was searching for water." John sounded delighted.

He'd been searching for water. He'd found water. It took her a moment to realize exactly what this was. "Hot springs!"

Immediately she fantasized about a good, long soak—the perfect remedy for her tired, aching muscles. But not every hot spring was safe for humans.

"Have you checked the temperature?"

"Yes. The springs originate farther up the mountain." He pointed, but in the dark Kerry saw little. "The water is too hot there, but this pool feels about perfect. A hundred and four degrees, I'd guess."

Oh, that did sound heavenly. "But what about chiggers?"

"There isn't much vegetation. Kerry, in the light the pools looked really clear. And the water's about three feet deep. Coming in?" John was already untying the laces on his boots.

Kerry thought of her poor, throbbing foot. The hot water would be so therapeutic. The rest of her body would benefit from a good soak, too. It had been days since she'd been able to enjoy a proper wash.

"Oh, yeah. I'm coming in." She dispensed with her boots, her clothes, her underwear, too. For a moment she paused, her attention on John. His naked body was magnificent in the pale moonlight. Her paler skin, she feared, must make her look like a ghost in comparison.

"Come." John held out a hand to her, then led her into the deliciously warm mineral water. If muscles could sigh, hers did in that glorious moment of submersion.

"Ah! It's perfect...." Using her hands to feel her way, she found a submerged rock that made a perch for sitting. John did the same just a few feet away.

For a long moment she did nothing but close her eyes and enjoy. Then John said, "Let me massage your foot."

"You don't have to do that. This water is just what I need."

"Come on, Kerry. You've put in a lot of miles." He reached underwater, and soon she felt his hand grip the back of her calf. Reluctantly she let him pull her leg up until her left foot was resting on his thigh.

This wasn't the first time John had seen her foot, but she was still sensitive to its slightly deformed shape—the inward curve of her sole, the twisted angle of her toes.

"You don't need to do this, John."

But his hands felt so wonderful she didn't drag her foot away. Instead, she relaxed.

"Remember that time we tried to follow your parents' map when we were kids? We thought it would lead us to a real treasure box filled with gold and diamonds."

It was the first time he'd referred to the trip that had been so much in her mind these past few days.

"I think about it," she said. "And I remember how brave you were. Right up to the bitter end…"

IN THE DARK, clutching the back of Johnny's T-shirt, unable to see more than a flicker of light from the flashlight he held in his hand, Kerry felt more afraid than she'd ever been in her life.

"Maybe we should turn back." She hated to be the one to say it. But Johnny wouldn't. He was setting a pace that had her huffing.

"Don't tell me you're tired."

She was, but wouldn't admit it. "I'm hungry."

"Eat something from your pack."

"I would if you would stop for a minute."

Johnny let out a disgusted grunt. Stopping, he turned. "Satisfied?"

He waited while she rummaged around for a sandwich. The minute she had the plastic wrapper off, he began moving again.

"Hey! Where are you going?"

"Can't you eat and walk at the same time?"

"Let's set up camp for the night. It'll be fun. Maybe we could have a fire…."

"We can't have a fire, stupid. Then they'd find us for sure."

"Do you really think they're looking for us?" The idea was thrilling, in a way.

"Well, for you, anyway."

Another one of Johnny's strange comments that she couldn't understand and was beginning to know better than to question.

"What if they find us before we find the treasure?"

"They won't," Johnny said, and Kerry's uncertainty vanished, only to reappear as he added, "except this doesn't seem to be working out right. According to the map, we should've come to a creek by now."

That was worrisome. "Maybe it dried up." She'd heard her aunt and uncle talking about what a hot summer it was.

"Maybe." Johnny stopped. Not expecting this, she bumped into his back and dropped her sandwich.

"Oh, darn." She fell to her knees, searching for the soft bread and sliced turkey. In the dark she couldn't see a thing.

"Here." Johnny shone the flashlight for her. She was just reaching for her food when an eerie howling came from up in the mountains.

"Oh, Johnny!" After years of living on the Dumas ranch, she recognized coyotes when she heard them.

"Don't worry. They won't hurt you."

The first call was being answered by a second, somewhere over her left shoulder. Kerry forgot about her sandwich, the treasure, everything. It was one thing to listen to coyotes from your bed in your very safe bedroom. It was quite another to hear them out in the mountains in the middle of the night.

"Johnny, how much farther do you think?"

"I don't know." Suddenly he sounded as tired as

she felt. "I think maybe we're on the wrong mountain."

At that moment, another howl sliced through the night air. Not a coyote, she thought. "What was that? It sounds dangerous. Do you think it could be a wolf?"

Johnny played the beam of light on her face. Kerry winced, shaded her eyes. "Cut that out," she complained.

"That's Friday, my dog." He moved the light away from her face and onto the path.

His dog? Kerry felt a little foolish, then angry. "How do you know that's Friday? How could he have followed us so far?"

"My dad is using him to track us. Your uncle is probably with them."

Wow. That was impressive. "Can your dog really do that? Like Lassie?" On TV, the collie had found a missing child based on the smell of his sweatshirt, or something like that.

"Friday is way better than any mutt they've got on TV." Johnny shuffled the flashlight from one hand to the other. "Look, it isn't going to take them long to catch up to us. I think you should just head back."

Kerry scanned the path they'd covered, then ahead to where they had yet to go. Both choices seemed equally dark and unappealing. It was true she'd really wanted to find the treasure. But by now she was sure—and Johnny probably was, too—that they weren't looking in the right place.

So what was the point in going on? It was colder out here than she'd expected. And she missed her cousins and Aunt Eleanor and her cozy bedroom.

"Okay. Let's go back. We can search for the treasure another day."

Johnny's only answer was to stuff the map into her pack, then hand her the flashlight.

She stared at it doubtfully. "You want me to lead?"

"Yeah."

Wow. She hadn't expected that to happen. So pleased was she with her new responsibilities that it took her a while to realize Johnny wasn't following her.

Turning her flashlight on the path up the mountain, she tried to call him back. Crazy kid! What did he think he was doing? Did he want to find the treasure without her? But he'd given her the map.

Kerry's tummy ached with fear for her friend. She thought about the food he'd sneaked from the Dumas kitchen. About the secret he'd refused to share with her that afternoon. Finally, she realized that the treasure had been an excuse.

Johnny was running away from home. That had been his plan all along.

JOHN STARED into the star-sprinkled sky and thought about the moment when his father had caught up to him on that mountain. He'd been more sad than angry. And John had made a personal vow to never run away again, no matter how crazy his mother acted.

For the first time he'd realized that his father needed him almost as much as he needed his father. Only together could they survive living with the sort of woman his mother had become.

A week following their escapade, he and Kerry had returned the map to the drawer in her uncle's desk. They'd never mentioned the map or the treasure again.

He'd never believed in the treasure, anyway. It was running away that had appealed to him, though he hadn't admitted as much to Kerry.

"We had a lot of nerve, didn't we, John? For a couple of eight-year-olds."

"Yeah." They'd made quite the team. Then and now.

"John, why did you want to run away from home that day?"

"Why does any kid run from home?" John shifted his weight from one rock to another. In that quick space of a second or two, Kerry eased her foot off his thigh. "Maybe my father asked me to clean my room and I didn't want to. I really don't remember."

Kerry didn't buy that explanation for a second. "It was your mother you were running from, right? You just couldn't take her drinking anymore...."

Mention of his mother brought a familiar tightness to John's gut. For some reason, Kerry seemed determined to probe every difficult, painful topic she could find.

But he didn't want her to know about that side of him. He wanted her to remember the boy she'd played with on those long, happy days at the ranch. Not the miserable, unhappy creature he'd been in the Eagles' basic log cabin in the mountains.

He'd never loved her more than he did tonight, right this minute. She looked so beautiful sitting across from him, her delicate features tantalizingly revealed in the strained light from the moon behind constantly shifting clouds. He could hardly believe all she'd endured in the past few days. Her courage and strength amazed him. They always had.

"John," she asked gently, "how bad was it?"

And her tenacity continued to annoy him. "Drop it, Kerry. You really don't want to talk about this. Trust me."

Despite soaking in warm mineral water, his muscles were tensing with Kerry's every query. He tried to think of another topic of conversation, but Kerry forestalled him.

"Why don't *you* trust *me* for a change? I think it might be good for you to talk about her, John. Despite all her problems, she was your mother."

"She didn't deserve the title. You wouldn't know. You were raised by Eleanor Dumas. A woman who never forgot your birthday, who checked to make sure you brushed your teeth every night, who washed your jeans and even patched them when you tore a hole in the knee.''

He could have gone on for half an hour, listing all the little tasks he'd observed Eleanor Dumas doing for her children—and often for him, too—during those long childhood days on the ranch.

The woman hadn't been able to step out of the back door of her house without him tracking her every move—to the clothesline to hang out a load of laundry, to the garden to pick fresh produce for the next meal. Sometimes she'd come at a run when one of the kids had hurt themselves. She'd whisk the child indoors and wash and bandage the wound, kiss away tears, offer cookies in exchange for smiles.

She'd treated him no differently from her own. Perhaps she'd even spoiled him a little. And he'd soaked up the attention like a cactus in a desert rainstorm. Yet every night at home, he still felt empty inside.

''Eleanor is special,'' Kerry acknowledged. ''But not every mother can live up to that standard.''

''You know what bothered me the most? I know my mother's life was hard, but she didn't even try.'' He'd never voiced the thought to another person, not even his father. Especially not his father. But the question had festered in him for practically his entire life. Why hadn't his mother ever made an effort? To give up the booze, to put her life back together, to love her son and her husband?

Maybe he wasn't being fair. Maybe, on some level, she'd exerted herself. But he'd never seen any evidence of it. She sat in her room, watching TV, feeling sorry for herself and drinking whatever she could get her hands on. Toward the end, she wouldn't even eat anymore. Just whiskey, whiskey, whiskey. Even now, he hated the smell. The sight of an empty, dirty bottle on a street corner brought back that old lost, hopeless feeling.

"Tell me." Kerry leaned over to grasp his hand. Wholesome, strong, brave—Kerry was everything he could want from a woman. Everything his mother had not been. Everything he did not deserve…

"Tell me," Kerry repeated, reaching out with her other hand. He knew, even before he felt her touch, where she was headed. Tenderly she brushed the four marks.

"What happened here, John?" Kerry's words were softer than her fingers.

No. He couldn't. *Back off, Kerry,* he wanted to say. But somehow, the words that came out of his mouth were quite different.

"I was four years old, sitting at the table with my mother. We were having lunch."

He could remember how it had felt to be that age. His feet had hung from the edge of his chair, too short to reach the wooden floor. He remembered how his mother, already grossly overweight, had seemed so huge and overpowering at her place across from him.

"Your father?"

"He was outside doing chores. I'd finished what was on my plate, but I was still hungry."

Can I have some more? His mother hadn't answered. She was staring at her reflection in the metal toaster on the table. His mother always turned to stare at the sight of her own face—whether in a photograph, a mirror, a darkened window.

Was she mourning her lost beauty? Her forsaken opportunities?

"I reached for a slice of bread from the pile at the center of the table. My mother hadn't been paying any attention to me. But when she saw my hand move, she pounced, stabbing me on the back of my hand with her fork."

"Oh, John…"

He was still in that room, remembering. Funny how he'd fought so hard to forget that day yet was able to recall every detail so vividly and freshly. The look of satisfaction on his mother's face as she'd yanked the prongs from his flesh. The blood, dripping onto the finely textured store-bought bread, spreading in uneven circles. His father's cry as he'd unexpectedly opened the kitchen door and seen…everything.

"My father came in from his chores early. He saw what she did—and heard her yell at me for getting blood all over the kitchen table."

"Oh, Johnny…"

He wondered if Kerry realized she'd used his childhood name. It was the first time he'd heard it in years. No one called him Johnny anymore. A powerfully built six foot six, he suited John much better.

Still, the sound of that old name was familiar and sweet coming from Kerry.

He took a deep breath, and the scene from that day receded into the dark. Once more he was an adult. And the throbbing, bleeding gashes on his hand were only faint scars.

"My mother was drunk. She only hurt me when she was drunk."

"So there'd been other times?"

Kerry sounded as if she couldn't bear to hear about them. He shouldn't have told her as much as he had. Now she would feel sorry for him when there was really no need. He was an adult, talking about stuff that had happened over twenty years ago.

"She'd hurt you before, hadn't she?" Kerry asked. Unexpectedly, she put her hand on his shoulder, then trailed her fingers over the patch of bumpy skin below his left shoulder blade.

"Did she do this, John?"

Oh, hell. Why not confess, lay the whole sordid scenario at her feet? "Yeah."

"Oh, John… How?"

"She hit me with the iron." She'd *branded* him, like a young steer. He'd been even younger that time, and his father hadn't found out about the incident until many years later.

Something wet dripped onto his arm. Kerry brushed the moisture away with the palm of her hand. He tilted her chin, barely able to see her face in the moon's faint glow. Tears glistened on her cheeks, and a new droplet beaded in the corner of her eye.

He'd made her cry.

John sighed. "It was a long time ago, Kerry. And after the episode with the fork, it didn't happen again. My father never left me alone with her once he saw what she was capable of."

They were both naked, but Kerry seemed to forget or else she didn't care. She came to sit beside him and wrapped her arms around him, burying her face between his head and his shoulder, rubbing her warm salty tears like salve on his tough, dark skin.

"I'm sorry for crying. I know that makes you uncomfortable. Maybe I had no right to ask you those questions. But I'm glad I know. I wish I'd known sooner."

John sat very still, afraid to betray his body's response to her closeness. "You couldn't have stopped it. You were still with your parents when it was happening."

"Anyway, I wish I'd understood why you were so quiet sometimes. Do you think your father told Eleanor and Hamilton?"

"They probably guessed something wasn't right at home when my father started bringing me with him to the ranch every day. But I don't think my father ever told them specifically."

He wouldn't, would he? That wasn't the Eagle way. John respected his father for his stoic strength, and for the most part did his best to emulate it.

But today he hadn't been stoic. For the first time, he'd aired the family's dirty laundry—and felt surprisingly okay about it. In front of anyone else, these admissions would have made him terribly embarrassed. Kerry was different, though.

Because he loved her. Even if he shouldn't. He was very aware of her bare breasts against his chest, her thigh touching his. Only when she nuzzled her lips against the hard line of his jaw did he find the strength to move away.

"John... What's wrong? Don't you want to kiss me?"

He stood on legs that lacked their customary strength. She could see that he did want to kiss her, and more. But that wasn't going to happen. "We need to be careful not to stay in too long. The water's very hot, Kerry."

"I don't care about the water. John, you can't keep avoiding me. I know you want me."

Embarrassed at his body's betrayal, John shuffled through the water until he reached the edge. He stepped out and reached for his clothes, pulling on his pants first.

"You won't feel this way once you're in Reno." He turned his back so he couldn't see her follow him. Kerry's beautiful, athletic form, gleaming with water and moonlight, was too much for him to take. He listened to her shuffle into her waiting clothes.

"You're pretty sure about that, aren't you, John?"

She sounded angry. He wondered if it was because,

deep inside, she knew he was right. Resisting the temptation to argue, he remained silent as he led the way to their cave.

All that remained of their campfire were orange embers and ash. He crouched next to the fire and played with it—added more wood, poking around with a stick—while Kerry ditched her clothing one more time before easing into her sleeping bag.

He wondered if she would invite him to join her. But not another word passed between them. Soon she fell asleep. After the crazy day they'd had, she was undoubtedly exhausted.

But John wasn't tired. He rebuilt the fire, then sat for a long while thinking about his father and his mother and the terrible trap their marriage had been for both of them. And for him.

He couldn't do that to Kerry and any possible children. He wouldn't. When they got out of here, he was going to give his notice and move to another state. He'd make a new life for himself somewhere, and Kerry would slowly forget about him. She'd meet someone new, or maybe she'd change her mind again about this Evan. One thing, the guy had to be crazy about her to go to the trouble of renting a helicopter and chasing after her.

But if Evan Sutcliff was that enamored, then why had he let his fiancée take off into the desert by herself in the first place? There was something about this man, John decided, that didn't add up.

CHAPTER FIFTEEN

"Is THAT what I think it is?" John asked.

It was the eve of their third day trekking toward civilization. The sun hung low on Kerry's right. She blinked her sore eyes and squinted in the direction he pointed.

"I can't see anything." Lord, but she was sick of the sand. The grit was everywhere, from her eyes to between her toes. Even her tongue felt coated with the stuff.

"I think it's your car."

They'd calculated their route to take them to her Subaru. She had the keys in her pocket, and she squeezed them hopefully.

"Forest green?"

"I'm not sure."

Kerry kept moving out of sheer doggedness. They'd covered miles with John leading, her at his heels. Rarely did they talk, and what conversation they managed was about when to break and where to get water and how to best ration the supplies she had left.

Two nights ago John had snared a rabbit, but that

was the only food they'd eaten, other than her dried provisions and his tea, since they'd left the valley.

John's stubborn silence was maddening. Why was it that after finally opening up and confiding about his mother, he was treating her like a stranger? Worse than a stranger, because he couldn't even be bothered with small talk. All her comments about the weather, the wildlife, the beauty of the sky were met with grunts at best.

She could only imagine how he'd respond if she tried to speak about more meaningful subjects—like the way they felt about each other, and what they were going to do about these feelings once they returned home.

Kerry had lots of ideas, and she was dying to share them. Unfortunately, she suspected John's opinions wouldn't coincide with hers. If he had feelings for her—and she knew he did—he'd deny them.

He'd already told her what he thought. They were too different. She had more money, a better education. Most damning of all, she was white, his mother had been white and look what had happened to her.

John had convinced himself that once this adventure was over and Kerry was safely home, she'd change her mind about him. As far as she'd been able to figure out, there was only one way to disprove that theory.

And that was to get to her condo in Reno as soon as possible. Then maybe he'd believe she wasn't suffering from desert-induced madness when she said she loved him.

"I don't believe it." John's mouth hadn't curled in a smile for days, but it did now. Kerry caught her breath looking at him. He'd unbuttoned his shirt earlier, and she could see the smooth, deep-brown skin of his chest and belly. His wild, dark hair perfectly framed his strong, proud features.

"It's your car, all right."

Kerry wrenched her gaze from the man to the familiar profile of the vehicle she'd abandoned what seemed a lifetime ago. She'd worried vaguely about vandals, but her car looked exactly the same as when she'd left it—except for a thick layer of dust. She ran a hand over the hood, then inspected the tires. Everything appeared fine.

She fumbled with her keys, then finally forced them into the lock. Exhausted at the idea of driving over the rutted playa, she stood there until John took the keys from her hand and crawled into the front seat. First he moved the seat back, to make room for his legs, then he tried the ignition. The engine started without protest.

"Well, that sounds good." John emerged from the car. He glanced at her as if questioning why she wasn't in more of a hurry to start the drive back.

Predictably, he said nothing.

The last minutes of the day—the final ones of their adventure—were slowly running out. They stood— Kerry leaning against the car, John several yards away, framed by the desert sky—and watched as the sun sank below the horizon. Layers of pink and mauve darkened into the midnight blue of twilight.

Finally, John sighed. His boots ground against the sand as he walked toward her.

"It's time to go," he said. "Do you want me to drive?"

"Aren't you tired?"

"No."

He never was. At least not that she could tell. "All right, then." She tossed her pack in the trunk, then settled into the passenger seat. As soon as her door was shut, John shifted the car into Drive and hit the gas. The car responded perfectly, giving no evidence of having suffered for its week in the desert.

Kerry wriggled in her seat. When she'd begun this journey, she'd anticipated returning to wear Evan's engagement ring.

Now she knew it was something she could never do. The prospect of telling Evan this, however, was nothing to look forward to.

Still, she'd feel better once things were straight between them.

Cool air brushed through her hair as they gained speed. John had his window open, and every now and then he stuck his head out for a closer look at the stars.

"Should I get my compass?" she asked. On the playa there were no roads, no signs, no streetlights to aid in navigation.

"That's okay," John assured her. Those were the last words he spoke for the entire trip.

Kerry did her best to respect his desire for silence. John's quiet spells were nothing new. As a child she'd accepted them, knowing they never lasted longer than a day or two. Now she had a deeper appreciation for the causes of his withdrawal, and paradoxically a greater sensitivity to them.

Talk to me, John. Tell me what you're thinking. Kerry did her best to will his confidences, but eventually the dark, and the soothing vibrations of the car, lulled her to sleep. When she awoke, John was pulling into an unfamiliar driveway.

"Where are we?" She pushed her hair from her face and sat up straight.

"Friends of mine live here. This is where I left my Jeep. We're in Gerlach." As he watched her gradually become more alert, his eyes spoke more to her than his words, betraying emotions he would never own up to.

His vehicle, she noticed, was almost hidden by shrubs at the end of the drive.

"So this is where we part ways." She wasn't ready to leave him. She knew that whatever his true feelings were for her, John would fight them. And that would be easier for him to do once they were no longer together every minute of the day.

"Are you too tired to drive to Reno?"

If she said yes, what would he do? "It's not that far. I'll be fine."

"I know you will." He wasn't talking about the car trip, she guessed.

"Will you call me?" She hated that she sounded desperate. But she couldn't let him go without asking.

He shook his head. "Not a good idea."

"Damn it, John."

"You'll have Sutcliff…"

"That's over. How many times do I have to tell you?"

"Maybe you should try telling him first." Avoiding her gaze, he opened the car door and slid out. "I left my keys with my friends. Looks like they're home."

Lights shone from all the main-floor windows. She couldn't let him walk away like this. She jerked the car door open and ran after him, catching his arm before he had a chance to knock on the front door.

"You know I don't love Evan. I never did." *Look at me, John.*

"Once you get home—"

He turned to the door, forcing her to pull hard on his arm. "I don't even *want* to go home. Not if you're not there."

"Kerry, stop!" His voice was harsh, and she instinctively stepped away from him just as the outside lights flashed on. She saw his face clearly as he flinched from her gaze.

"Go home." He corralled her to the shadows at the side of the house. "It's the best thing."

The front door was opening. She had only a second or two. "Is that really what you want me to do?"

A woman stepped onto the front porch. Her blond hair was in a ponytail, and she carried a fussing baby in her arms. "John, is that you?"

"Goodbye, Kerry." He nudged her toward her car, then turned toward the beckoning light. "Hey, Karli. How's Blade Junior? I hope I didn't wake him. I was just seeing off a friend who gave me a lift."

A friend who gave me a lift.

Kerry reminded herself who she was all the way to Reno.

ON THE OUTSKIRTS of the city, Kerry zipped into a drive-through for a burger, fries and a thick chocolate shake. She ate as she drove, but the food wasn't as delicious as she'd anticipated. She tried not to think of John or to wonder whether he'd spend the night with his friends or drive straight to Carson City.

It was ten o'clock by the time Kerry let herself into her dark, stale condo. She turned on lights and opened windows, all the while convincing herself that it was too late to call Evan. She'd wait until morning, then see him at work.

She walked past the flashing red light of her answering machine, shucking her filthy, torn clothing, then balling it into the trash.

Naked, she returned to the kitchen, pausing first to glance in the hall mirror. Her bruises had mostly faded, but, Lord, was she dirty. Ignoring the faint stirrings of guilt as she passed her answering machine again, she opened a bottle of white wine she'd left chilling in her fridge. Fast food and Chardonnay—just the combination for how she felt tonight.

She carried the glass of wine with her into the bathroom, averting her eyes so she couldn't see the damn flashing light this time. She showered, watching the sand filter off her body in a gray stream, then she lathered her hair three times before she finally felt clean.

Next on the agenda was a bath. Oh, how she'd looked forward to this! She ran water, added bath oil, then turned on her radio. Listening to a favorite tune by Sarah McLachlan, she realized how accustomed to quiet she'd grown during her days in the desert. Easing into the tub, she sighed with satisfaction.

This felt great, it really did. No way was she going to let thoughts of John spoil the moment. So what if he didn't want to be with her? He wouldn't fit in this tub, anyway. He was too tall. His feet would dangle over the edge.

Fighting the remembrance of him rubbing her foot in the hot springs, she slid deeper into the fragrant water. Head leaning against the tub, she let that first sip of wine slide down the back of her throat. This was heaven, and she couldn't be happier. Tonight she was going to sleep in a real bed, with clean sheets and a plump, fluffy pillow. She'd have a cup of civilized Earl Grey tea and maybe read for a while, if she could keep her eyes open.

Evan, a nasty voice at the back of her mind reminded her. She was going to have to deal with him eventually. It wouldn't be pleasant, she was afraid. Frankly, the fact that he'd hired a helicopter and scoured the desert to find her didn't fit with the man she thought she knew. They were affectionate with each other, but that sort of action implied a passion she'd never sensed in him. Where had it come from?

On reflection, maybe it would be a mistake for her to speak to Evan at work. She wasn't due in until the following Monday, after all. Perhaps she could call him tomorrow afternoon and suggest they have that dinner he'd sounded so keen on.

Would John call? She didn't know why she bothered to wonder. He wouldn't. There wasn't a chance.

She took another sip of wine, then another, trying to relax. Damn it, she'd been out in the desert for over a week. She'd earned this bath; she was going to enjoy it.

And yet, five minutes later she was out. Dripping wet, wrapped in a towel, she jabbed at the playback button on her machine, then listened, scowling.

Ten messages. All of them from Evan, urging her to call the minute she set foot in the door. "I've been so worried. All I want is to know that you're okay."

She was erasing the last of them when the doorbell rang. Kerry stared at the entrance to her condo blankly. Her first crazy thought was *John.*

Then sanity returned. Her visitor was probably the neighbor she'd asked to keep an eye on the place while she was gone. Kerry dashed to the bedroom for her robe. Even though she knew, she just *knew* that John wouldn't be standing in the hall waiting for her, her heart pounded as she opened the door.

"Kerry!" It was Evan, looking as if he'd roused himself from bed only minutes ago. "Why didn't you call?"

She stepped away from his embrace, tightening the belt on her robe. "I haven't been home long. And I only just checked the machine." That she hadn't planned on phoning him at all this evening was information she chose not to share.

Suspicion warped the smile on Evan's face. He scanned the room behind her. "He's here, isn't he? That half-breed boy you grew up with. I saw him from the helicopter, even though you tried to hide. You have an awful lot of explaining to do, Kerry Dumas."

"Nobody is here."

Evan brushed past her, checking the bathroom, bedroom, kitchen, before finally ending up in the living room.

"Did you look under the bed?" Kerry planted her hands on her hips, not hiding her annoyance.

"Where is he?"

"I don't know. Probably at his place in Carson City."

"Why didn't you tell me he was going on this trip with you?"

She didn't drop her gaze. "I didn't plan to meet up with him. It just…happened."

Evan scowled and shook his head disbelievingly. "You expect me to buy that?"

"I know it sounds…unlikely." At the very least. "But I still don't understand why you came after me in that helicopter. I told you how important this trip was to me."

"What choice did I have? You weren't honest with me, Kerry. Like why you wanted to take that trip in the first place. You were looking for something specific, weren't you, Kerry? Did you find it?"

Kerry froze. She'd never told Evan about the map or her conviction that her parents had died while on a quest for something important.

"I found my mom and dad's wedding rings," she said cautiously. "And I think I have a clearer understanding of why they passed away in that desert."

Evan frowned. "They died of exposure and dehydration. Just like anyone would if they were trapped in the Black Rock without supplies. That's why I was so worried about you. Why didn't you call?"

"Unfortunately I broke my radio." She held back the details of her fall. Evan didn't seem all that concerned about her safety. His first questions hadn't been about her welfare at all. But about John. *And the meteorite.*

"I'm sorry I caused you concern."

"And I'm sorry if I overreacted. It's just that I love you so much."

He tried to hug her again, and this time she took his hands to stop him. "I'm afraid I don't feel the same way, Evan. You deserve better, I know…"

Having drawn certain conclusions about John's presence in the desert, Evan wasn't completely taken aback, Kerry could tell. Still, he set his jaw, preparing to argue. "This isn't the right time to make that decision. You can't—"

Staring at his familiar face, Kerry realized that she had no idea what he cared about. Why had she ever felt she knew this man well enough to contemplate marrying him?

Suddenly she was very anxious to get rid of him. "It's late, Evan, and I'm exhausted. I think you should leave. We'll talk about this another time, after we've both had a chance to think things through."

"Kerry, I don't want to go. I want to know what happened to change your mind about me. You told me when you came back you'd wear my ring."

Kerry would have felt badly if he'd seemed unhappy or sad. But all she sensed from Evan was frustration and anger. "I'm sorry, Evan. I didn't want to tell you like this. I'd planned to wait until I was rested."

But he'd had to show up at her door, uninvited. "By the way, how did you know I was home?"

He stared at her for several moments before finally responding. "I was returning some movies and noticed your lights were on."

Kerry shivered. She knew where he lived and the

store he rented his videos from. Her home was definitely not on the route. He'd been watching. Waiting.

A jealous lover, desperate for his woman to return? Or something more?

"You have to go now, Evan. I'll call you later."

Before he had a chance to react, she closed the door in his face and bolted it, then ran to her phone.

She *had* to talk to John.

"HE'S GONE *WHERE?*" Kerry heard the words clearly enough, she just couldn't believe them. John and two others from the sheriff's department had taken a helicopter into the desert.

The information hadn't been easy to come by. She'd traced him through a series of connections starting with her cousin Zach and ending with the receptionist at the sheriff's office. She hung up the phone, dazed by what she'd been told.

This morning she'd opted to take the remaining days of her two-week vacation and not return to work. She'd tried to get through to John but had received the same recorded message she'd encountered when she'd attempted to phone him last night. Hadn't he even gone home to shower before heading into his office?

Or checked his phone messages? But then maybe he had and was avoiding her call for a reason.

She thought guiltily of Evan, who had phoned twice this morning and whom she'd callously put off. He was playing the role of brokenhearted suitor, but she couldn't forget his questions about her trip. He knew something, but how? She needed to talk to John.

But John obviously didn't want to talk to *her*. To think she'd considered him a friend, a lover, a soul mate. And he was treating her like some mistake he'd picked up at a bar and wanted to forget.

Why hadn't he discussed his plans to return to the mountains so quickly? He'd had plenty of opportunity during their long hike to the car and the drive to Gerlach.

The phone rang, and Kerry pounced. But it wasn't John on the line, it was her godmother, Deanna. Kerry had phoned earlier that morning and left a message.

"Kerry, darling, it was wonderful to hear from you."

Deanna had been her mother's closest friend. They'd roomed together in residence during their university years and stood up for each other at their weddings.

"Deanna, I have a question for you. It's kind of important."

"Well, sure, honey. How can I help?"

"Do you remember a man named Brian Henderson? I think he may have known my parents." She didn't add that she and John had found his skeletal remains in the high desert not far from the place where her parents' bodies had been recovered so many years ago.

"Oh, Brian. Yes, of course, your parents knew him. They worked together for several years."

"Brian Henderson was a geologist?"

"Among other things," she said vaguely. "He actually went to the same university as us. You'll laugh at this—he dated Susanna until your father came along."

"Hmm." Funny, no. Interesting, yes.

"It took Brian a while to get over being dumped, but eventually the three of them became fast friends." Deanna paused, and when she continued, her voice was thoughtful. "His family reported him missing not long after your mother and father died. I always thought it was a peculiar coincidence. What made you ask about him after all these years?"

Kerry told a portion of the truth. "I've been getting these memory flashbacks. And one was of being in his helicopter."

"That's right—Brian loved to fly. I'm sure the experience must have been memorable for a child. Tell me," Deanna asked, veering off topic, "how's that young man of yours? Any chance I should be marking a day off on my calendar to come to your wedding?"

Gently, Kerry indicated that the relationship was over. After promising to call again soon, she hung up, anxious to think about what she'd learned.

As a geologist, Brian must have suspected what her parents were looking for when they began their trek into the desert. Supposing he'd set out into the desert, too, and caught up to them after they'd found the meteorite. Perhaps he'd attacked her father when he refused to tell him about the secret passage. Or maybe the two men had fought over her mother.

In either scenario, her father had been pushed over that ledge and broken his leg, and her mother had done her best to take care of him. Meanwhile, Brian had attempted to find the passageway on his own—and failed.

Kerry paced as she thought, trying to control her excitement. Everything fit, she was certain she was right, but what she wanted was someone to go over the facts with. Someone being John, of course, but he was currently not available.

And probably wouldn't want to speak to her even if he was.

Kerry ordered in pizza for dinner that night. She had another shower—she couldn't seem to get all the sand out of her hair—then watched sitcoms. It wasn't until almost nine that Zach called with information from his contact at the sheriff's office.

"The helicopter landed about an hour ago. Apparently the men were recovering some human remains John found when he was backpacking in the desert a few days ago. Know anything about that, Kerry?"

"I'll fill you in later," she promised. "Have they identified the…remains?"

"The deceased was a white male in his thirties," Zach told her. "A Brian Henderson. They've already notified next of kin. His sister and her husband are flying out tomorrow morning."

"One more thing, please." Kerry took a deep breath. "Is John back in the office? Did you talk to him?"

"John?"

There was a pause, and Kerry heard some muffled conversation in the background.

"Sorry, Kerry, but apparently John didn't come back with the others. I guess he's still out in the desert."

CHAPTER SIXTEEN

KERRY KNEW where to find John and she was determined to go to him as soon as possible. But good sense dictated that she prepare for this trip as cautiously as she'd prepared for the first.

She cleaned out her backpack, washed her sleeping bag and outfitted her flashlight with fresh batteries. After a quick lunch she went shopping for a new radio and food supplies, then had her car refueled and serviced. By the time she arrived home, it was clear she wouldn't be leaving until first thing the next morning.

She got up when her alarm went off at dawn, indulged in an extra-long shower, then dressed and ate breakfast. On her way out the door, she almost tripped over the morning paper. She was about to toss it aside, but the cover photo and headline grabbed her.

Remains of Missing Man Found in Desert. Kerry unfolded the front section and spread it on the kitchen counter. A photo of a couple in their sixties had been captioned, ''A twenty-five-year-old mystery is finally solved for the sister and brother-in-law of Brian Henderson, a geologist whose remains were found in the Black Rock Mountains two days ago by Deputy Sheriff John Eagle.''

Kerry's gaze lingered over her former best friend's name for a moment, then she glanced at the photo. She could've sworn she'd seen this couple before, but no matter how hard she focused, nothing specific came to her. Giving up, she turned to the article. In the second paragraph, the couple's name hit with a jolt.

"Cara and Walter Sutcliff flew in from Dallas to claim the remains for burial."

Two words glared from the gray newsprint. *Sutcliff. Dallas.*

Kerry froze as the implications sank in. She *had* seen this man and woman before. In a photograph in a brass frame on one of Evan's end tables. She knew his parents lived in Dallas, Texas. His parents were Cara and Walter, Brian Henderson's sister and brother-in-law.

Oh, dear Lord. She had been dating—had contemplated marrying—the nephew of the man responsible for her mother's and father's deaths. This could *not* be a coincidence.

Despite the early hour, she dialed Evan's home number and unsurprisingly caught him in bed.

"Kerry?" His voice was husky. "Why are you calling so early? Is something wrong?"

It was hard to know where to start. "Brian Henderson was your uncle."

He cleared his throat, then she heard the rustle as he tossed aside his bedcovers. "If you'd answered your phone yesterday, I would have told you that. My parents are in town—''

''I know. I saw their picture in the morning paper. Evan, don't you think you should have told me?''

''You never mentioned finding my uncle's remains out in the desert.''

''If I'd known he was your uncle, I would have!''

''Well…''

He couldn't come up with an excuse, because he didn't have one, damn it! ''You moved to Reno to find out what your uncle had been searching for in the desert. You dated me because you knew Brian Henderson was a friend of my parents.''

She didn't have any romantic feelings for Evan anymore, but still it made her angry to know she'd been used.

''That may be how it started. My parents had this crazy idea that my uncle died during a search for some priceless artifact. I was supposed to find out what you knew. But I fell in love with you instead. Then you told me you wanted to go backpacking through the desert on your own. I didn't know what to think. I thought maybe my parents had been right all along.''

''And that's why you hired that helicopter. Not because you were worried about me but because you wanted to know what I'd found.''

''I *was* worried about you.''

And yet, practically the first thing he'd asked her when she got back from her trip was what she'd found. "I don't believe you, Evan. And I don't want to speak to you ever again."

"This isn't fair…you kept your share of secrets from me. You never told me the real reason you wanted to go on that backcountry trip to the desert or that you were planning on meeting that half-breed. You had a map, didn't you? Kerry, if you found something, you owe it to me and my family to tell us."

Did Evan have any idea what his uncle had done to her parents? Not that she could prove it, but in her heart, she knew what had happened.

"I owe you zip, Evan. And you may be right that I wasn't open with you. But you're the one who first introduced deception to this relationship."

Kerry hung up the phone because, really, what else was there for either of them to say? At this point, sorting through all Evan's lies would be impossible. All she knew for certain was that he was the last person she wanted to know about the meteorite.

IT WASN'T until he finally trekked to his cave that John took the time to think about the phone message that had been waiting for him when he'd hurried home to shower and change before heading into the desert.

The call had been from Zach. He'd admitted he'd worked things so Kerry and John would meet that first night in his cave.

"Probably I should have just minded my own business,'' Zach had admitted. ''But truth is, I've never felt Sutcliff was the right guy for Kerry. You may think I'm nuts, but I always thought maybe the two of you...''

Something had interrupted Zach then. There'd been a one- or two-second pause, then he had concluded in a rush, ''Anyway, call me when you get back and I'll buy you a beer. We'll talk.''

With a click, the call had been disconnected. John had been in too much of a rush to phone his friend at that time. He'd already been in touch with his office and arranged for a helicopter to retrieve the body in the mountains.

John did his best to remember, word for word, what Zach had said. *I always thought maybe the two of you...*

Was it possible Kerry was right? That her family wouldn't be opposed to the idea of them as a couple? From the sounds of that phone message, Zach wouldn't be.

Of course, the Dumases were broad-minded people. He and Kerry would run into prejudice from lots of other sources. But did he really want his life dictated by the opinions of people who thought that way?

John unrolled the sleeping bag he'd brought with him. He'd given up on his crazy notion of a spirit quest. He didn't need a dream to tell him what to do. And he knew, too, that he was wasting his time puzzling over Zach's phone call.

By now, Kerry was thanking her lucky stars she

hadn't made a commitment to him. She and Evan were probably dining at a posh, romantic restaurant this very moment.

Closing his eyes, John told himself to sleep. Kerry wasn't his to worry about, and she never had been. Tomorrow he'd hike his way out of the desert and start that new life he'd planned.

New Mexico. Texas. Didn't really matter. As long as he put plenty of miles between himself and Kerry Dumas.

Sleep nabbed him in the middle of that thought, and he slept deeply for hours. Then suddenly he was in the middle of a dream that was more vivid, more real than any he'd experienced in his life.

He was the brave in his grandfather's legend, the one whose profile was carved in the rock that had fallen from the heavens. Around him were people from another time, strangers...only the closer he looked, the more familiar they became.

Sitting on the ground, grinding berries between two rocks, was a beautiful woman. His mother. No longer sick, alcoholic and old, but young and healthy. She smiled at him with a warmth he'd never seen on her face before.

Several dark-skinned women buzzed around his mother, sharing her work. The women were talking together, laughing frequently. *They accept her,* he realized. *Even though she's white.*

His father was here, too, and his grandfather. They stood among a group of men craning their necks at the sky, frowning, murmuring. As John turned his gaze upward, he felt the temperature drop and heard the keening of a new and powerful wind. In the heavens, a haze swirled around the sun. Day darkened to twilight in less than a minute.

The elders barked out orders to the tribe. It was time to move on. Men and women abandoned their daily activities to pack belongings. Children were gathered; food and clothing were bundled. As the sense of impending disaster swept in with the billowing wind, John clasped his hands uselessly. He desperately wanted to help these people, to travel with them. But he was frozen in place. Aside from that smile from his mother, none of the people around him acknowledged his presence in any way.

He tried to catch the eye of his grandfather.

What's happening to me? Why can't I move? I want to help you....

Desert sand swirled around him. The gray sky blackened. A terrible noise, a howling, shrieking wind blocked all sound from his ears. Everyone was gone. He stood alone.

Wait, my son.

His grandfather's words rose over the wind, then sank into the surrounding mountains. Confused, John stood his ground while the world around him became an alien wasteland.

Grandfather... What am I waiting for?

KERRY.

John rubbed his eyes and looked again. It was Kerry, all right. Standing at the entrance to his cave just as she had almost two weeks ago. Only this time she wasn't here because of her parents' map. She'd come to find him.

And suddenly he knew exactly what his grandfather had meant when he'd counseled him to wait.

"Are you okay, John?" She approached, kneeled beside him, brushed her palm over his forehead. "You feel hot."

"I had a dream." He pushed himself into a sitting position and accepted the water bottle she offered. The dream had been like none he'd ever experienced before, yet in some ways it felt more real than life itself.

His mother had been whole, his father happy. Suddenly John could remember details that hadn't been in his first version of the dream. He saw himself at four, at six, at ten. He recalled hunting and fishing with his father and grandfather, stories and songs from his mother. A lifetime of memories—too much for just one dream.

And his hands. Thinking back to the moment when he'd been frozen in place, unable to run like the rest of his people, he remembered wringing his hands. And they'd been smooth. No scars.

He touched himself, and felt the familiar four bumps. Of course he felt them. Did he think they would have disappeared? God, he must be crazy to have thought that.

Yet the memory of how he'd ended up with those

marks was more vague. Instead of seeing his mother's cruel smile of satisfaction, he heard her soft crooning at night, something he'd never experienced in real life.

"John, tell me your dream," Kerry urged.

He opened his mouth but couldn't find the words. Was this how his grandfather had felt after having one of his visions? Up until now, John had been skeptical. The real world was what counted.

But last night, he'd been offered a choice. A different kind of past and a different future, too.

"What are you doing here, Kerry?" Afraid his dream might have taken another surreal twist, he touched her cheek, her hair, her shoulder. As much as he could be sure of anything right now, he was sure of her.

"Looking for you, of course. I drove up to the mountains and parked in the same spot as before. From there, it was just a five-hour hike. But you know that."

She picked up a stick and played with the dying fire. "John, why did you come back here? And why didn't you tell me?"

"I had things to figure out." Like, did he really believe he wasn't good enough for Kerry Dumas? That's what it would have boiled down to if he'd quit his job and moved, tail between his legs. If his grandfather had been alive, John might have sought his advice. Instead, he'd done the next best thing and sought refuge in his cave.

Wide awake and sober, he felt that through his dream he had visited the old shaman. Perhaps he had more native blood in him than he'd ever admitted.

Kerry's bold blue eyes were shaded with doubt. "But you came in a helicopter. With two other men..."

"Only to recover the body. I *did* tell you we'd have to do that, remember? Don't worry, we didn't go near the tunnel to the valley."

The stress lines around her eyes vanished. "I'm glad to hear that. I don't want that rock dissected and studied, or thousands of tourists trekking over these mountains."

He couldn't agree more. That they felt the same about this only confirmed what he'd known for so long. He and Kerry belonged together.

"As for Brian Henderson," she continued, "he made the front page this morning. His family flew up from Dallas to claim his remains. And guess who his sister just happens to be? Evan Sutcliff's mother."

"What?" John listened in amazement as Kerry explained the connection and Evan's original purpose in moving to Nevada.

"I think Evan always hoped I knew more than I was letting on about what my parents were searching for in the desert."

And she had. But that was information she'd never

shared with her almost-fiancé, only with John. He held her secrets, just as she held his.

The need to touch her again was irresistible. This time he kissed her gently on her mouth, then traced a line down her arm and captured her hand.

"What's going on?" Kerry asked, eyes wide, lips moist. "I thought we were all wrong for each other."

"Does this feel wrong?" He dipped his head, found her mouth again and kissed her with passion.

Kerry cupped his face between her hands. "John, it feels wonderful. But what made you change your mind?"

How could he explain? "Many things. A phone call from your cousin. My dream. Finding you here when I awoke. Kerry, for a long time I've been confused. But now everything is absolutely clear."

His quest hadn't been to forget Kerry, but to love her. It had taken a coyote, a dream and a rock from the heavens to show him the truth.

And, right on cue, a coyote howled. John absolutely *knew* it was their trickster. Kerry did, too.

"I think he approves of that kiss you just gave me," she said. "For the record, so do I."

"I love you, Kerry. I want to be with you always." He felt reborn, revitalized and full of hope. And he knew he could make Kerry happy, keep her safe, give her the children she craved. Children he so desperately wanted, too.

The legend was about belonging, about home, about love. And with Kerry, he'd found all three.

Look forward to all these
★ wonderful books this ★
Christmas ★

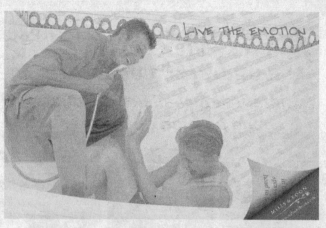

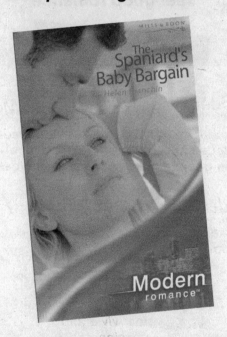

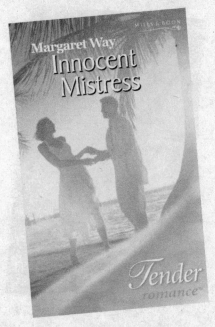

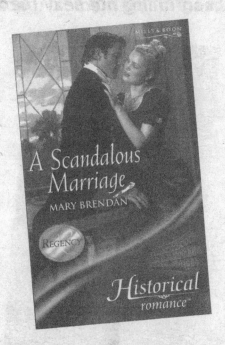